KILL ROMMEL

In this clever mix of fact and fiction, John Kerrigan starts a major new series detailing the rise of the SAS over half a century to become the world's most élite formation.

North Africa, 1941: General Rommel, the commander of the German *Afrikakorps*, is marching on Cairo. Churchill decides he must die. The task of assassination is given to Colonel Geoffrey Keyes. But Keyes has a dangerous rival, Captain David Stirling, the founder of the Special Air Service (the SAS) who is seeking fame for himself and his unit. Who will carry out the murder, Keyes or Stirling?

KILL ROMMEL

KILL ROMMEL

by
Leo Kessler writing as
John Kerrigan

Magna Large Print Books
Long Preston, North Yorkshire,
England.

British Library Cataloguing in Publication Data.

Kessler, Leo writing as Kerrigan, John
   Kill Rommel.

A catalogue record for this book is
available from the British Library

ISBN 0-7505-1041-2

First published in Great Britain by Severn House Publishers
Ltd., 1995

Copyright © 1995 by John Kerrigan

The right of the author to be identified as the author of this
work has been asserted in accordance with the Copyright,
Designs and Patents Act, 1988

Published in Large Print 1997 by arrangement with Severn
House Publishers Ltd.

Magna Large Print is an imprint of
Library Magna Books Ltd.
Printed and bound in Great Britain by
T.J. International Ltd., Cornwall, PL28 8RW.

Author's Note

When the papers of Major Rory O'Sullivan DSO, MC turned up so surprisingly in a Belgian flea market just off Brussels' *Grand Place*, SAS HQ in Hereford was caught completely off guard. Before the Director of the SAS could react and obtain them for the Regiment, they had already been sold.

It was something that the Director didn't like. Ever since the SAS was secretly reformed after World War II (probably at Churchill's orders—he always had a soft spot for the Regiment), the top brass of that unit have always been exceedingly careful about what they let the general public know about the Regiment's activities.

Even now, ten years since the 'O'Sullivan Dossier' (as the papers are now being called by military historians) turned up so surprisingly, no one has explained convincingly how they came to be sold at the Belgian flea market. Some authorities have maintained it was an act of revenge on the part of Major O'Sullivan's estranged Belgian wife, la Comtesse de Manderfeld. They state she wanted to embarrass and

7

hurt the O'Sullivan family by showing that they had been involved in covert and sometimes unpleasant secret operations for the SAS for three generations. After all, these authorities reason, the Countess couldn't have expected to make much money on a Belgian flea market, could she?

Some suspect that the KGB was behind it all. At the time young O'Sullivan, Rory O'Sullivan's grandson, was killed in action he had been fighting the Yemeni communist-supported rebels. This was something that was known only to a few people in Britain. A disclosure of this kind, so some authorities feel, would have acutely embarrassed the British government of the day. Others maintained that the CIA, which was definitely supporting Israel at the time, wanted the Arab connection to be revealed and show they had no part in the Yemeni business.

Indeed the 'O'Sullivan Dossier' raises many questions and provides—sadly—few answers. And by the time Rory O'Sullivan's papers came into the possession of the present author some of the more sensitive operations in which the O'Sullivan clan were engaged had been removed from them, such as the SAS's role in Vietnam, a very hot potato indeed. And one doesn't need a crystal ball to know who removed those sections of the 'Dossier'.

But what remains is very powerful stuff even so. The 'Dossier' provides a unique insight into the workings of the SAS since its founding, for the O'Sullivans were—and are (for there are still some of them serving with the Regiment)—an SAS dynasty. The late Rory O'Sullivan seems to have collected *everything* that linked his family to the secretive elite regiment ever since its foundation in 1941.

Not only are there recorded facts, relating to ops, that the general public has never heard about, but also the artifacts of the time: invitations to the wartime Kit-Kat club in Cairo, a rude letter from Paddy Mayne (four DSO's) to the then prime minister just before his death; a picture of a ceremonial dinner at the Duke Street Drill Hall, London in 1950, with the signatures of at least four commanders of the Regiment, including that of its founder, 'the Phantom Major', David Stirling.

The 'Dossier' makes it quite clear just how ruthless David Stirling was in putting his new regiment 'on the map', as he always called it. How he actively, desperately, sought that first great mission which did exactly that, but which resulted in the death of the first O'Sullivan to die in battle with the SAS, killed in action at the age if nineteen before he had begun to live.

The 'O'Sullivan Dossier' details that secret and unknown SAS mission to France in September 1944 which was betrayed to the Gestapo by the French Resistance with terrible consequences for the captives. And how, after the war, with the SAS officially disbanded a group of them went to wreak revenge on the traitors.

In essence, the story of the O'Sullivans is the unofficial secret history of an elite secret organization which has changed the nature of military tactics and which has been imitated throughout the world from Russia to the United States.

But let us start at the beginning. 1941 in the Western Desert, a certain young captain of the Brigade of Guards hobbled quite illegally into the GHQ at Cairo on crutches, dodging both sentries and staff officers alike, to put forward a revolutionary new idea...

John Kerrigan, Spring 1995

PART ONE

A Mission Is Proposed

'When I die, bury me face down.
That way the whole damn army
can kiss my arse.'

The Sayings of Paddy Mayne,
SAS 1941–1945

Chapter One

'Yes,' Captain Gore-Smythe said grimly, 'that's the bastard! There's no doubt about it. That's him all right.' He rubbed his right hand, covered with dried blood, across his forehead wearily. 'I've seen him in the cinema newsreels. It's him.'

O'Sullivan looked at the company commander. Normally Gore-Smythe never swore, but he supposed it was the strain which made him do so now. They had been on the run for forty-eight hours now, ever since most of the company had been wiped out near Bardia. All of them were wounded and they were nearly out of water. O'Sullivan told himself the Captain had good reason to curse.

The heat was intense. The desert sun struck their eyes like a sharp knife. But lying in the hot white sand, the four survivors of 'A' Company, Second Battalion, the Grenadier Guards, noticed neither the heat nor the glare at this moment. Their attention was fixed on the little convoy of German armoured vehicles which had come to a halt on the desert road some hundred or so yards away from their hiding place.

A group of officers had descended from them and were peering through their binoculars to their front—the way the Eighth Army had retreated—while a circle of soldiers in the peaked cap of the *Afrikakorps* stood guard, machine pistols at their ready.

But the watchers' gaze was fixed not on the soldiers or the officers with their glasses. They concentrated their attention on the officer standing to one side of the group. He was medium-sized, older than the rest and, despite the terrific heat, was clad in a long leather coat and he wore the cap of the regular army, not the peaked one of the *Afrikakorps*. Even at that distance O'Sullivan could see the look of ruthless determination on his pugnacious face with its formidable cleft-chin. The man positively radiated power and drive.

Shielding his eyes with his wounded right hand, Gore-Smythe stared at the lone figure in the leather coat and said grimly, 'That's the Hun who destroyed our battalion, perhaps even the whole of the Brigade for all I know. That one Hun has been keeping us on the run ever since he and his damned *Afrikakorps* arrived in the Western Desert.' His bronzed unshaven face, pared down to the bone by the

14

hardships of the last weeks, hardened to stone.

'But who is he, sir?' Guardsman Dawson ventured. He was a giant of a man, well over six foot two, who had been in the King's Company before the war. Now his wounded left arm was supported by a sling made of his web-belt and he had a dirty shell dressing, stained with black blood, around his forehead.

'The Desert Fox... Field Marshal bloody Rommel,' Gore-Smythe snarled. 'The cause of all our troubles.'

'Sir,' O'Sullivan whispered.

'Yes, Bill,' the company commander said, not taking his eyes off the lone figure for an instant.

'Don't you think we should scarper, sir? They're going to turn and look this way soon.'

Gore-Smythe turned for a moment and looked at O'Sullivan, with his emaciated face and the desert sores on his chin. God, he thought, O'Sullivan's only a kid, nineteen, but he's already been through Dunkirk and a six month tour in the Western Desert. Tough as they come, yet only a kid really, not long out of short pants. 'Yes, I think you're right, Bill. You're in charge now. Better slope off before they do spot us.'

O'Sullivan looked puzzled. 'I'm in

charge, sir? I don't quite understand.'

The company commander gave him a weary smile. 'Sorry, Bill, but I'm sick of running. Besides I can't go on any further. My leg's giving me too much gyp.' He indicated the bandage covering his shattered knee cap. 'I'm staying behind.'

'We can carry you, sir,' Dawson whispered. 'Me and Smith 175 here.' He indicated Guardsman Smith, one of the twenty Smiths who had been in the battalion before it had been wiped out— hence the last part of his army number to distinguish him from the rest. 'Can't we, 175?'

'Course we can, sir,' Smith 175, who had been shot in the throat, croaked loyally.

Gore-Smythe laughed drily, 'A bunch of old crocks like you lot!' he mocked. 'Can't ruddywell carry yourselves by the look of it.'

'But, sir,' O'Sullivan protested.

'No buts, Bill,' the Company commander cut in sharply. 'I'm giving you a direct order, you're to leave now. Head due east, keeping the coastal road to your left. I reckon what's left of the brigade will have pulled back to the Wire'—he meant Libya's border with Egypt—'probably as far as Sollum. I should imagine with what you've got left in your water bottles you

16

can make it—with luck—in twenty-four hours.'

'And you, sir?' O'Sullivan queried, looking very worried at the thought of abandoning the captain.

Gore-Smythe tapped the butt of the service rifle he had been carrying, taken from the body of one of his dead Grenadiers. 'I've got a score to settle, Bill. That Hun over there wiped out my company. I think it's about time I did the same to him.'

'You mean Rommel, sir?' O'Sullivan gasped, his lean handsome young face aghast.

'Yes, why not? I'm a crock now with my knee. I'll never see active service again. Might as well do something useful. Kill Rommel and we'll knock the whole of his damned *Afrikakorps* for a six, I bet.'

'But they won't let you get away with it, sir,' O'Sullivan protested hotly, mind racing electrically, as he considered whether he shouldn't order the two guardsman to seize the CO, and take him with them whatever he said to the contrary.

'I don't suppose they will,' he answered with a weary smile. He turned to his front and picked up the rifle. 'Goodbye, Bill.' There was an air of finality in his movements and O'Sullivan knew there was no further use in protesting.

'All right,' he said to the two big guardsmen, 'we'll crawl back to that big dune. Once we've covered by it, we'll be able to move faster.'

For a moment it looked as if the two of them might refuse to obey his order, but then the rigid discipline of the Brigade of Guards took hold once more and crooking their rifles across their arms, the two guardsmen started to slither through the burning sand towards the dune to their right.

O'Sullivan hesitated. Gore-Smythe seemed to sense the young man's hesitancy for he said without looking round, 'I said, goodbye, Bill. Better be off before the balloon goes up.'

'Goodbye, sir,' O'Sullivan said sadly and then he, too, had cradled his rifle in his arms and was crawling after the others towards the dune.

Behind him, Gore-Smythe raised his rifle and peered through the sight. Rommel's hard powerful face came into foreground, in between the two metal prongs of the sight. Gore-Smythe pushed back the bolt and loaded. He took aim again. Rommel's face suddenly wavered and swam before his eyes. He felt himself becoming faint. He knew why. He was exhausted and had lost a lot of blood. 'Dammit,' he cursed and, blinking his eyes, forced them to clear. Rommel came into focus again. Carefully, very carefully, his finger started to curl around the trigger of the rifle as he started to take first pressure.

One hundred and fifty yards away, Rommel swished away the importuning flies with his fly whisk. *'Scheissfliegen!'* he cursed. He hated the desert with its flies, its desert sores and heat, but he knew that it was there that he would make his reputation. There were a good half dozen German field marshals fighting in the snowy wastes of Russia. But their names and deeds remained relatively unknown to the German public. In Africa it was different, because here the Anglo American press had made a kind of hero of him. Hadn't they nicknamed him 'the Desert Fox'? That had been a nickname that had gone right through Germany. My God, thereafter he had had hundreds of admiring letters from the Homeland, including a score or so from women who offered him their bodies. He grinned slightly at the thought.

But as he stared eastwards towards Egypt and the enemy, he knew he must not let the campaign drag on for ever. The Führer wouldn't continue sending him men. Hitler needed every soldier he could find for the hard pressed

Eastern Front. The *Afrikakorps* had to beat the English for good soon or else...

'*Herr Generalfeldmarschall*' the harsh voice cut into his reverie sharply.

He swung round. It was *Oberfeldwebel* Dahmen, who was in charge of his body guard. 'What is it, *Oberfeld?*'

Dahmen, a huge man with hard dark eyes, pointed by way of answer. 'Out there in the desert. Something just flashed. Perhaps glass.' He shrugged and lifted his machine pistol.

As one the officers and Rommel raised their glasses and focused them on the sand shimmering in the blue afternoon heat so that even with binoculars it was difficult to make out objects.

Rommel was the oldest man of the group, but he was first to spot the intruder. 'There's a man out there,' he cried, 'armed with a rifle!'

'Those damned Arab Senassi,' one of the staff officers, yelled in alarm. 'They're always taking pot shots at us and the Italians.'

Dahmen acted at once. He was taking no chances. 'Down, Herr Rommel,' he ordered. 'You, too, gentlemen. At *once!*' He turned to his group of burly military policemen, with the silver gorget of their calling around their throats, 'All right,

20

don't stand there like a pot waiting for piss. *Move it!*'

As the officers crouched, feeling rather foolish as they did so, the military policemen, strung out in a line, started to advance on the man lying there on the desert floor, weapons clenched in their big fists...

The single shot rang out like a twig snapped under foot in a dry summer. O'Sullivan stopped in his tracks and Guardsman Smith 175 said, 'It's the CO sir. He's done it—'

The angry burst of machine gun fire followed by a shrill scream of absolute, unbearable pain drowned the rest of his words. The scream seemed to go on for ever. Then there was a loud echoing silence.

O'Sullivan looked grim. Has the CO pulled it off? Had he shot the Desert Fox? He didn't know. But one thing he was certain of. Gore-Smythe had paid the penalty for his bravery. He was dead whatever he had achieved or not. 'Come on,' he said finally. 'They might be looking for us soon. Let's hoof it.'

They 'hoofed' it: three big men trudging stolidly across that burning empty waste, as if they might well be the last men alive. But even as he led his little group of survivors, moving one weary leg after another by an effort of sheer naked willpower, those words of Gore-Smythe kept echoing and re-echoing through his mind. *'Kill Rommel and we'll knock the whole of his damned Afrikakorps for a six...'*

Chapter Two

'We're all going, if our CO's will let us,' Hastings of the Scots Guards chortled happily, ignoring the fact that he could only walk with a cane. 'Heaps of us from the Brigade. Others as well. Paddy Mayne from the Commandos. He used to play rugger as a forward for All-Ireland. Fitzroy MacLean, who used to be an MP. All jolly good types and dead eager. It's going to be a jolly good show, what!' He smiled happily at Bill O'Sullivan, who still had his wounded arm in a sling.

It was early 1941 and now a month since what was left of the 22nd Guards Brigade had pulled back to Cairo to wait for new equipment and reinforcements to fill the great gaps in its ranks. During that time O'Sullivan, in company with the rest of the wounded officers had been patched up and discharged from Cairo's General Military hospital to make way for the new casualties who were coming in every day.

For a while he had sampled the fleshpots of Cairo and there were plenty of them—the Lido, the Kit-Kat Club, the bar at Shepheard's Hotel, the *feluccas* rowed out into the night on the Nile, with women of easy virtue. But by now O'Sullivan was getting sick of the Egyptian capital, the reek of the river, the pot-pourri of dust, dried dung and Arab cooking, the noise which went on all night. He longed to get back to the front, with all its dangers.

Now he said, 'Hold on Stephen, who's all volunteering and what kind of jolly good show is it going to be?'

Hastings looked at him, as if he were an idiot. 'Don't you know, Bill?'

'Of course I don't, or I wouldn't bloody well have asked.'

Across the road from the Hospital, where they had just had their wounds dressed, an Arab in a dirty white robe was beating a skinny-ribbed donkey, laden down with a great pile of firewood, as if he intended to beat it into the ground with his stick. Barefoot children with flies crawling into their nostrils and men in striped pyjamas eating cold white beans out of bowls watched him with little interest. It was as if they were more interested in who would give in first—the donkey or its owner.

'Perhaps you recall David Stirling? He

used to be with the Scots Guards, but he volunteered for the Commandos,' Hasting said, ignoring the donkey which was braying piteously under the blows from its owner; he was too much concerned with his own affairs.

'Yes, I think I do,' O'Sullivan said slowly. 'Big fellow with a heavy jaw?'

'You can say that again,' Hastings agreed promptly. 'Six foot five in his cotton socks. Well, after his particular commando was disbanded he looked around for another bunch of irregular warfare wallahs. But there were none. So he decided to form his own unit.'

'He did what?' O'Sullivan gasped in disbelief. 'Captains don't go around form-ing their own units, not in the British Army they don't.'

Hastings chuckled. 'You're right there, but you don't know David. He dodged into GHQ and button-holed no less a person than the Commander-in-Chief himself, and y'know, the old boy gave him permission to start L-Force.' He beamed winningly at the younger man. 'Really brass-necked, what?'

'But what is this L-Force, whatever that means, going to do?' O'Sullivan asked in some bewilderment.

Hastings laughed so that a group of VAD nurses passing out from the hospital looked at him sharply, as if he might have been one of their 'bomb happy' patients who had managed to escape from the secure ward. 'Make bloody merry hell, if I know David Stirling, Bill.'

O'Sullivan's mind raced suddenly. Across the street the donkey lay on its back, its load shed, panting in quick shallow gasps, as if it might die at any moment, while the owner stared down at it in a puzzled kind of way as if he couldn't understand why the beast was suddenly lying there. The barefoot boys and the men eating cold white beans continued to watch in silence, perhaps waiting to see how long it would take for the animal to die.

'Are you game, Bill?' Hastings cut into his reverie. 'David is meeting would-be volunteers in the bar of the Shepheard at twenty hundred hours tonight. If he likes the cut of your jib, he'll take you, I know. But first you've got to get your CO's permission.'

'Great Scott.' O'Sullivan's handsome young face fell suddenly, 'I hadn't thought about that. Old Colonel Peter's not going to take this very well I'm afraid.'

Across the road, the skinny-ribbed donkey had died. Now its owner was staggering off, bent under the great load of firewood, while the little boys with their nostrils full of flies had produced knives from somewhere and were busily sawing at the beast's carcass. The men in pyjamas had seen enough. They retired to their seats in the shade and, with their beans eaten, started to suck at their bubble pipes in apparent contentment. It had been a good morning's entertainment...

'Sit down, Bill,' Colonel Peter Cousins, the officer commanding what was left of the Second Battalion of the Grenadier Guards, said a little wearily.

Outside on the dusty parade ground, a sergeant major was bellowing, as if he were back at Pirbright, 'Swing them arms! Bag of swank. I know you all think you're ruddy battle-hardened veterans, but I've shat better veterans than you shower before breakfast. Open them legs now. Nothing'll fall out and if it does, I'll pick em up fer yer.' He chuckled coarsely. 'Now come on you bunch o' pregnant penguins, swing them arms!'

'Before I forget,' Colonel Cousins said, 'I must tell you you've got your gong. The War Office has approved your MC. Congratulations, my boy. I had to wait till I was twenty-two before I got my first Military Cross.'

'Thank you very much, sir,' O'Sullivan said. He knew 'Pop' would be very proud of him. At the same time he felt even

26

more of a rat now. The Colonel had recommended him for the country's third highest award for bravery and he was about to ask for a transfer.

He looked at the CO and thought he had aged ten years since he had first been posted to the Second Battalion. There were bags under his eyes and his face, yellow with jaundice, was lined and worn. He looked more like forty-five than thirty-five.

'Now then, Bill,' the Colonel said, trying to appear brisk and alert, 'Where's the fire, my boy?'

'Sir, I'd like to apply for a posting. To Captain Stirling's new L Company...' He broke off. The Colonel's face had fallen suddenly. Then it had turned an angry red.

'What did you say, Bill?' he barked.

O'Sullivan repeated his request.

'But dammit, Bill,' Colonel Cousins snapped, 'You're my most experienced junior officer now. Soon we'll be flooded with raw replacements from Blighty and I'll need all the experienced men I can find to train them and make them ready for battle.'

'I know that, sir,' O'Sullivan said miserably. 'But it's exactly because of that I've decided to join Captain Stirling if you'll let me go.'

Cousins kept a grip on his temper with

27

obvious difficulty. Outside the sergeant major was bellowing, 'Slow march...now keep them arms to yer sides. Come on now...head up. Yer not looking for frigging half crowns in the gutters...'

'I know this man, Stirling, Bill,' the Colonel continued. 'He moves with a fast group, Randolph Churchill and that lot. They're always out drinking and gambling beyond their means in Cairo's flesh-pots. Stirling has no idea of admin. He's never really seen any kind of action in three years of war. What kind of chap is he to raise a new unit?' He puffed out his yellow cheeks in scarcely concealed exasperation.

'But sir, we'll be training the new boys for months on end. My guess is that we and the rest of the 22nd Guards Brigade won't see any action till next year. And that's too long for me. I want to have another crack at the Boche as soon as possible.' O'Sullivan's handsome young face hardened, 'After what they did to the battalion last month.'

'Laudable, Bill. Laudable. But how long do you think a unit run by a bounder like Stirling will last? They hate his guts as it is in GHQ.' Colonel Cousins tried another tack. 'Now Bill,' he said, trying to be reasonable, 'you know there have always been O'Sullivans with the Grenadiers. Your great-great grandfather fought with us at

28

Waterloo. His son was at Inkermann during the Crimean War with the Grenadiers. Your grandfather fought with us in the Boer War. Your father served with my father in the trenches as a subaltern in the last show.' He looked hard at the young officer. 'With a bit of luck if this war lasts long enough, you'll be commanding a company, perhaps even the battalion. You can't throw all that away, all that family tradition, simply to join that mountebank Stirling, surely not.'

O'Sullivan bit his bottom lip. He understood the colonel. Pop, his father, would be terribly disappointed when he found out he intended to leave the Grenadiers. But he was, all the same, determined to see action again as soon as possible. Listening to the sergeant major ranting on the square outside made him even more determined.

He knew what the Second Battalion would be doing for the next three or four months. They would be drilling and even more drilling. That was the way of the Guards and he didn't want to waste any more time on ceremonial drill. 'Sir,' he said, trying to keep his voice from quavering, 'do I take it you are turning down my request for a posting?'

The colonel shrugged. 'Oh all right,' he snorted, 'have it your way. You can go,

O'Sullivan. But I will tell you this for free. You'll regret joining that cad Stirling till the day you die—and with him in charge, that may be very soon.' He waved his hand in dismissal and bent his greying head to his papers. He did not even look when O'Sullivan saluted and went out.

'*Sir,*' O'Sullivan blinked hard in the sudden glare of the blood red sun. On the square the young guardsmen were lathered in sweat, as the sergeant major, big, brass-shod pacing stick clasped rigidly under his right arm, as if he were back on parade in front of Buckingham Palace, put them through their paces.

'Sir,' the voice hissed again.

Surprised O'Sullivan turned round.

Smith 175 and Dawson, both with their small packs slung over their backs together with their rifles, crouched in the shadows with something of a furtive air about them. 'Permission to speak, sir?' Dawson hissed.

O'Sullivan, still upset from his encounter with Colonel Cousins, said without interest. 'Yes, what is it?'

Dawson, casting an anxious look to left and right, as if he were afraid someone might overhear him, whispered, 'We've heard you're going to join this new mob under Captain Stirling of the Scots Guards.' He sniffed a little contemptuously at the mention of their rival regiment.

'Yes, I am,' O'Sullivan answered, puzzled why the normally loud-voiced Dawson was speaking in a whisper and why the two of them were carrying their rifles and small packs. 'What of it?'

'We'd like to go with you sir.'

'But you can't,' O'Sullivan protested. 'You haven't got a posting.'

Smith 175 winked knowingly. 'We don't need none, sir,' he said in a hushed voice, eyes on the grim-faced sergeant major at the edge of the square, ' 'cos we're deserting.'

'You what?'

'We're deserting, 'cos we can't face any more of that bullshit,' Dawson added his voice to Smith 175's and nodded at the sweating young soldiers on the square. 'I've done all the bullshitting I ever want to do, sir. If it moves salute it, if it don't paint it white,' he added mockingly, using the old soldier's phrase. 'I joined the Army to fight, not to blanco my webbing.'

O'Sullivan thought for a moment. This new unit would need seasoned soldiers like Dawson and Smith 175, as well as officers. He made his decision. 'All right then, you two rogues. But don't let the sarnt major see you or you'll be on jankers for the rest of your natural born days.'

'Ta, sir,' they said as one.

31

Five minutes later they were marching down the road to Cairo, with Smith 175 happily singing, 'We're off to see the wizard, the wonderful wizard of Oz.'

Up front O'Sullivan was not so happy at his escape from conventional regimental life. Indeed he felt decidedly sombre. For the first time he realized he had severed ties, not only with the regiment, but with nearly a century and a half of family tradition. Now he was entering the unknown and it was a decidedly funny feeling.

Chapter Three

They were standing at the far end of the big bar at Shepheard's Hotel, most of them Guards officers plus a few from the infantry, listening to Stirling tell them what he intended for his new unit. Overhead the fans stirred the air lazily and white-robed attendants wearing red fezzes buzzed back and forth bringing and serving ice-cold drinks.

O'Sullivan studied his new commanding officer. As Hasting had said, Captain Stirling was a huge man. He had a slight stoop but those eyes of his, under the beetling eyebrows, radiated urgency and confidence—perhaps a little too much confidence in himself, O'Sullivan thought.

He was saying in that slightly booming voice of his, 'there will be no bragging or swanking in thc Cairo or Alexandria bars and that goes for scrapping as well. Any energy you have for fighting will be directed at the enemy, please remember that gentlemen.' He took a hefty swallow from his glass of whisky. He nodded to the older officer standing next to him, 'Captain Jock Lewes here will be in sole charge of training and that includes my own. It's going to be tough because we have to be fit for the job we're going to do. If anyone has sensible and constructive comments to make on training, then make them. We are all here to learn. Is that understood clearly?'

There was a murmur of assent and O'Sullivan told himself that although he had not quite taken to the big Scots Guardsman, he liked the way he talked. He was very direct.

'Now as soon as we finish here we shall be off—'

He stopped suddenly. A huge officer, as big as himself, but even broader, had pushed his way into the throng. He was unshaven and not wearing his service belt. Behind him trailed two other officers in the

Balmoral and black hackle of the Scottish Commando. Both were wearing pistols.

'Paddy Mayne,' Hastings standing at O'Sullivan's side whispered, 'and he looks as if he's in a foul temper. Watch for fireworks.'

But when the big Irishman spoke his voice was quiet, though there seemed, to an interested O'Sullivan, to be an underlying snarl about it. 'My name's Mayne... Blair Mayne,' he introduced himself, staring hard at Stirling's face, as if searching for something there, which he found. 'And I've just been put under close arrest,' he indicated the two embarrassed young officers with him, 'for striking my CO.'

Someone whistled softly and there were muffled mutters of surprise.

At O'Sullivan's sides, Hastings said, 'Good God, he's punched Lieutenant Colonel Keyes, his CO. That's put the kybosh on it. Only last week he was supposed to have chased the colonel out of the officers' mess with a bayonet.'

O'Sullivan was impressed. In the Brigade of Guards, he told himself, they would have probably put you in the Tower of London for the rest of your life if you had struck your commanding officer.

Stirling took Mayne's statement in his stride. Swiftly he repeated what he had already said to the other officers, while

34

Mayne listened, no expression visible on his craggy tough face. But when Stirling was finished, Mayne said a little contemptuously, 'I can't see any prospects of real fighting in this scheme of yours.' Now there was undisguised scepticism on his face.

'There isn't,' Stirling agreed, 'Except against the enemy.' It was a clear reference to Mayne's recent exploit.

Mayne laughed suddenly. 'All right, if you can get me out of this, I'll come along.' He thrust forward a hand like a small steam shovel.

Stirling ignored the hand. He said, 'There's one more thing. *This* is one commanding officer you never hit—and I want your promise on that.' Then he reached out his hand.

'You have it,' Mayne answered. He smiled and O'Sullivan knew he was going along and was glad of it, for he saw that Mayne was going to be a pillar of this new untried unit.

'All right then, gentlemen,' Stirling raised his glass in toast. 'We'll be off to Kabrit on the Bitter Lakes which is going to be our training ground and camp. First thing we'll do is to learn how to parachute.' There were a few gasps at that. No one had ever learned to parachute in the Middle East before. The nearest training camp

35

for the newest arm of the British Army, the parachute battalion, was in Ringway outside Manchester, a thousand or more miles away.

'Now let me tell you the new name of the L Detachment,' Stirling continued as if he hadn't heard the gasps of surprise, 'and I'd like you all to drink a toast to it.'

All of them raised their glasses expectantly and hurriedly someone shoved a glass of neat whisky into Paddy Mayne's huge paw.

'Here's to the SAS,' Stirling intoned solemnly.

'The SAS,' Paddy Mayne cut in sharply before the others could respond to the toast. 'What the bloody hell is that?'

'*The Special Air Service*—the newest unit in the British Army,' Stirling replied. 'Now cheers.'

'To the Special Air Service,' the officers responded a little hesitantly.

'Sounds like a ruddy bus company to me,' Hastings whispered to O'Sullivan. Then he drained his glass. Sixty minutes later they were on their way out into the desert.

Behind them they left the two young officers of Mayne's escort drinking a little moodily at the bar (Stirling had done some quick string pulling at GHQ to have the big Irishman released to his custody).

'What do you think?' one of them asked after a while.

'About what?' the other said.

'I mean this SIS lark?'

'SAS,' the other corrected him. 'What do I think about it?' He sniffed and considered for a few moments while he stared down at his nearly empty glass, wondering as he did so whether he dare risk another one. Colonel Keynes was a bit of a prude when it came to drinking. 'Not much,' he said. 'I mean they're all like Paddy, totally bonkers. And I wouldn't trust that big fellow—Stirling—with a ten bob note. No,' he said, taking a final swig of what was left of the scotch, 'they won't last till Christmas. Come on, Phil, let's sling our hook or the colonel'll have his monthlies...'

'Kabrit,' Stirling announced, as they clambered stiffly out of the ancient Bedford trucks, which were the new unit's sole transport.

'Cor ferk a duck,' Smith 175 gasped when he looked around, swiping at the flies which seemed to be everywhere in the sudden heat of a new dawn. 'Is this it?' Like the rest he stared aghast at the new home of the Special Air Service.

It consisted of three tents, sagging in the middle, their canvas holed and dirty.

Stirling smiled ruefully, 'All I could

wangle from GHQ, chaps,' he explained. 'The one in the middle is my command tent. It's got a table and a wooden chair.'

'No bloody mess tent,' Mayne growled, rubbing his muscular right arm slowly, as if he might well be about to punch somebody hard. 'And where's the cookhouse?'

Stirling looked at the big, black-bearded Irishman a little nervously. 'It'll all come in due course,' he said. 'However, if there's any urgency in the matter, there's a New Zealander camp a dozen miles from here and the Kiwis have no supply problems at all. Their government sees to that.' He lowered his voice significantly. 'Don't say I told you, but the Kiwis are away in the desert on a scheme at the moment. Their camp is empty.' He looked significantly at Mayne.

'A nod's as good as a wink,' Mayne said and swinging round to face the other rankers standing behind the officers, 'I think we're going on a little jaunt tonight, lads.'

Their faces brightened and Smith 175 said, 'I hear them Kiwis get real butter and they've got beer, too. It comes in tins.'

O'Sullivan grinned and said, 'Do you mind if I come along Mayne?'

The big Irishman looked at him and evidently liked what he saw for he said, 'All right O'Sullivan—and I damn well

38

hope you're not a Catholic with a name like that—you're on.'

'Remember,' Stirling warned, 'I know nothing of this if you're nabbed.'

Mayne gave the CO a scornful look. 'Those Kiwis'll have to get up earlier in the morning if they want to nab Mrs Mayne's handsome son.'

The other ranks laughed and O'Sullivan told himself, he was beginning to like the SAS...

They returned at midnight that same day. O'Sullivan slid from behind the wheel of the overladen three tonner truck and said to the waiting crowd, 'All right chaps. Give a hand. We've got one or two goodies, including a crate of ice cold *Rheingold.*'

'Christ almighty!' Hastings exclaimed, '*Beer*—ice cold beer! Well, I live and breathe!'

'The Kiwis do themselves very well,' O'Sullivan said as both officers and men started to unload the gear they had stolen from the empty New Zealand camp, laughing crazily as they did so, chortling, 'God, look at this—real sheets...and mirrors, they've got frigging mirrors...' and 'I'll go to our house, wicker frigging chairs.

Half an hour later they squatted in their tents, filled with the furniture stolen from the Kiwis, the men drinking the *Rheingold*

39

beer, the officers passing round two bottles of Egyptian-made 'Victory Whisky'.

All were happy and slightly drunk. Someone somewhere was singing, 'Kiss me good-night, sarnt major, tuck me up in my little bed. We all love you, sergeant major...'

Stirling looked round the circle of flushed happy faces in the hissing white light of the stolen petroleum lantern. His new officers looked a good, tough bunch. He told himself they'd go to hell and back, if they were given the right mission. And he would make sure that they would. But at this moment, a moment of minor triumph at the way they had been able to loot the Kiwis' camp, he knew that he had to kill their euphoria. He had to lay down the ground rules.

He passed the whisky bottle to Paddy Mayne and said, 'Now, gentlemen, that was the first and last piece of organized looting by the SAS.'

Paddy Mayne frowned but said nothing. Instead he took a tremendous swig of the Victory Whisky before passing the bottle on to O'Sullivan.

'Well done,' said Stirling. 'We now have a respectable camp. Now I don't want to see it at a lesser standard than it is now. From now onwards our standards of dress and discipline will be every bit as high as those of the Brigade of Guards. I want a high grade of performance in everything we do. Remember GHQ will be watching us—critically—all the time. Those bloody staff wallahs don't like us one little bit. They'd be only too glad to close our shop up if they get the slightest chance. So while we're here at Kabrit, we'll give them a top notch performance. When we go on ops, things will be less formal. But there'll be some time to go before then.'

He looked around the circle of happy young faces, flushed a little by the cheap Egyptian whisky, their shadows magnified grotesquely in the flaring light of the lantern. 'Is that understood?' he asked, but even before they murmured their assent, he knew that they would back him up to the hilt.

'Well, gentlemen, that's it. I think we better ought to turn in. Training starts tomorrow morning at zero five hundred hours—sharp. Isn't that right Jock?' Stirling asked.

His second-in-command nodded his agreement and drained the rest of his whisky.

O'Sullivan followed the rest into the night and shivered a little in the sudden cold. Above, the stars cast their icy silver light on the desert. Suddenly he felt happy—happier than he had been for a long time. He didn't know why.

Over in their tent one of the drunken rankers was still singing about his 'sarnt major' who was 'like a muvver to me bringing up a nice hot cup o' tea...'

'Put a sock in it!' Paddy Mayne roared and the voice died away immediately.

Silence fell on the little camp buried in that remote desert. The SAS had ended its first day as a military formation.

Chapter Four

'Now, I know virtually nothing about parachute training,' Jock Lewes shouted against the wind which was howling across the desert, with camel thorn and sand whirling across its surface. 'So I'll have to make it up as I go along. I'm hoping we'll get the manual from Ringway sooner or later.'

He steadied himself on the back of the ancient three ton truck, its engine already running. 'What I'm going to do is to jump off the back of the Bedford as soon as the driver reaches fifteen miles an hour—then jump off into a backward roll. I've already tried the forward roll,' he added, 'and it hurts.'

'Cor ferk a duck,' Dawson breathed to Smith 175. 'A frigging backward roll at fifteen frigging miles an hour! That don't sound like frigging happy landings to me, mate.'

'You'll get one demonstration,' Lewes shouted, 'then you do it. All right, driver.' He slapped the canvas with the flat of his hand and the truck started to move off.

The observers heard the driver change into second gear, as the truck started to gather speed. The driver put his head out of the cab and yelled, 'Fifteen miles an hour, sir.'

Lewes didn't hesitate. He flung himself off the back of the truck. He hit the desert in a flurry of sand, rolled backwards and lay there for a moment, before rising, knocking off the dust from his uniform to say with one of his wry smiles, 'Easy as falling off the back of a lorry.'

Now as the days passed, the men of the new unit were subjected to a kind of training of a like they had never known before, even the regulars. They marched twenty miles in four hours, carrying packs laden with stones and under strict orders not to touch a drop from their water bottles. They learned how to operate in fours, each man of the foursome becoming an instant

43

specialist—in navigation, first aid, bomb-making, driving and mechanics. Sometimes they marched the night through, with not a drop to drink, nor anything to eat (and Lewes made sure that they didn't by searching them before they left) until they collapsed through exhaustion at dawn.

'Train hard and fight easy,' Lewes maintained always, to which Smith 175 would invariably reply (under his breath), 'I don't think I'll survive to fight. The frigging training'll kill me first!'

Two weeks after they had arrived at the remote desert camp, they were offered their first chance of jumping. An ancient Bombay bomber had been placed at their disposal. A hole had been cut out at the bottom of its fuselage, through which they would drop. But as the RAF dispatcher warned them. 'For Christ's sake, don't look down before you jump. Because if you do, you'll be needing a set of false choppers. The clout you'll get from the side of that hole will be terrific.'

Stirling went first, followed by Lewes and Mayne. Then it was O'Sullivan's turn. He looked down at the ground sliding away beneath the big lumbering ex-bomber, which dragged its black shadow behind it on the desert floor. Then he remembered the dispatcher's warning and jerked his head up sharply.

The dispatcher slapped him on the shoulder and shouted, *'Go!'*

Then O'Sullivan flung himself out of the plane. Suddenly his blood turned to water. He was hurtling down at a tremendous rate. The chute wouldn't open, he knew. He was plunging to his death. Abruptly there was a sharp crack. For a moment it seemed his shoulders were being ripped off. Then that crazy descent stopped, and he was floating down gently, with no sound save the faint hiss of the wind.

For the very first time O'Sullivan felt the exhilaration of the parachute drop. It had something almost sexual about it—a euphoric, but gentle excitement that made the nerve ends tingle. Then he forgot the euphoria and concentrated on his shroud lines, tugging them to empty the air out of his canopy, which he did successfully so that he landed on his feet with hardly a noticeable impact.

Next moment Smith 175 was rolling on the ground twenty feet away, crying with delight, *'The frigging thing opened...the chute opened!'*

Within the week they had all done their eight jumps which qualified them to wear the blue and white wings of the trained parachutist on their arms, their only casualties, Smith 175 and Dawson, who had both sprained their ankles.

'Just our bleeding luck, sir,' Smith 175 complained when O'Sullivan went to visit them in their tent to tell them that half the men and two officers had been allowed a forty-eight hour pass in Cairo, after the completion of the parachuting course. 'I ain't had it for so long I wouldn't know where to put it any more.'

O'Sullivan grinned. 'Well, next weekend the second half of the—or—the SAS,' he still found it difficult to use the name of their new unit, 'will get a forty-eight hours. By then you'll be OK.'

Dawson beamed up at him from his bedroll. 'Sir, I'll get there even if I have to get there on frigging crutches.' He grabbed the front of his shorts dramatically, 'Bloke needs a bit of the other now and again, or he'll go blind from bashing his bishop.'

Again O'Sullivan grinned. 'I don't think that'll happen just yet. Anyway the CO says he's going to bring back some *Rheingold* beer for the likes of us who are staying behind.'

'You, too, sir?' Smith 175 asked.

O'Sullivan nodded. 'Yes, I've landed duty officer for this weekend.' He grinned, 'All right, carry on.'

'Thank you, sir,' they said and Smith 175 added, 'no frigging carrying on in here, sir. Good-night.'

46

O'Sullivan was half dozing in Stirling's admin tent when the phone shrilled. He had been thinking of the last moments with Gore-Smythe, with the latter's words running through his mind: *'Kill Rommel and we'll knock the whole of his damned Afrikakorps for a six, I bet'*, when the ringing of the phone brought him back to consciousness. He grabbed the receiver and snapped. 'Duty officer here.'

'Is that something called the Special Air Service?' a harsh official voice demanded.

'Yes,' replied O'Sullivan.

'Well, this is the Provost Marshal's office, Cairo. And we're holding an officer who claims to belong to you. Do you know him? His name is Mayne—Blair Mayne.'

O'Sullivan gasped. 'Yes, yes, I know him,' he answered hurriedly. 'But what has he done?'

'What *hasn't* he done?' the voice at the other end snorted indignantly. 'Just wrecked a Greek bar and put six Aussie soldiers in the dock. One of 'em isn't supposed to regain consciousness till to-morrow at the best.'

'Oh my God,' O'Sullivan breathed. Although he didn't know the details, he knew only too well, a combination of strong waters and Paddy Mayne's explosive temper usually ended in trouble.

47

But six Australian soldiers! 'What can I do?' he asked hurriedly, collecting himself.

'Well, we've got him under close arrest. But we can't keep an officer behind bars indefinitely. Besides the Aussies are busy at this moment burning down Cairo's red light district. You know their crap. "Me old dad did it in the last war" the unknown speaker mimicked an Australian accent bitterly, ' "I'm gonna do it in this one, cobber. Are yer game?" So we're expecting a lot of business in the next few hours. We want to get shut of your Mr Mayne. Can you fetch him?'

'Well, we've only got one three tonner—and that's in Cairo at the moment.'

The man at the other end whistled, 'What kind of bloody unit are you? Only one three tonner.'

'Well, we've only just been formed. But our CO is in Cairo himself at GHQ. I'll call him and see if he can't bring Mayne back with him,' O'Sullivan said. 'Would that be all right?'

'I suppose,' the Provost Marshal's officer said hesitantly. 'But don't make it too long. He's already asking for bloody whisky and threatening to tear two cells to pieces if he don't get it. I've got six redcaps with truncheons standing by—just in case. So make it snappy.'

'I will. I promise you' O'Sullivan agreed hastily, 'and please tell Mayne to put a sock in it or the CO'll have him returned to his unit,' he added.

'Who in hell's name would have him!' the man at the other end said cynically. The phone went dead.

O'Sullivan breathed out hard. Then he set about dialling Stirling's number at GHQ, praying as he did so that the CO wouldn't lose his temper with Mayne. Paddy Mayne was a holy terror, he knew that well enough, but the Special Air Service couldn't afford to lose fighting men like him, even if they did occasionally wreck Greek bars and put six Aussies into dock.

The three tonner arrived back, together with all the leave men, at dawn the following morning. O'Sullivan, watching it arrive, told himself Stirling must have flown into a rage at Mayne's conduct and had ordered all the leave men back although they still had another twenty-four hours' leave to come. He bit his bottom lip and waited as the truck braked to a stop. The tailgate was let down and the leave men, hollow-eyed and unshaven, dropped to the sand stiffly.

Mayne was with them. Now he sported a black eye and the knuckles of both his big fists were bruised and red. 'Bloody

Mick Aussies,' were his first words as he approached an anxious O'Sullivan. 'Roman candles—the lot of 'em. And that slimy Greek bastard of a café owner, as well. I should have sorted him out while I was at it.' He clenched his fists and looked down at them, as if he were ready to lash out at any moment.

'Forget the Aussies and the Greek,' O'Sullivan said urgently. 'What's the CO's mood like? I see he's ordered the whole lot back. Didn't you—'

'What's the CO's mood like,' Stirling interrupted him in that booming voice of his, a happy grin spread all over his face, 'I shall tell you what the CO's mood is like, Bill. It's happy, very bloody happy.' He beamed at the younger officer.

Hastily O'Sullivan snapped to attention and flung Stirling a smart salute, saying, 'Good morning, sir.'

'And good morning to you, Bill,' Stirling said heartily. 'All right, Bill, let's have a bit of wakey-wakey.'

O'Sullivan looked at his watch and said, 'But it won't be reveille for another thirty minutes, sir.'

'Forget it, Bill. Regulations have just been tossed out of the window as of now. Give them the old "hands off yer cocks and on with yer socks business",

Bill.' His smile broadened even more and he flung out his hands so that for one moment O'Sullivan thought Stirling might embrace him. 'We've got a mission...'

Chapter Five

It was an hour later. Now they were all gathered before Stirling's admin tent, smoking or drinking tea from battered enamel mugs, waiting excitedly for Stirling's briefing to commence.

It was a beautiful morning, not too hot but the sun was hot enough to dispel the usual desert night chill and O'Sullivan felt good. Even his desert sores didn't itch this morning—and he was excited at the prospect of action soon. Besides him Smith 175, his ankle strapped up, a 'Woodbine' cocked out of the side of his mouth, said, 'And the Old Man,' he meant Stirling, 'needn't think he'll keep me out of this show just 'cos I cocked up the jump and hurt me frigging ankle, sir.'

O'Sullivan laughed and said, 'Rest assured, Smith 175, we'll take you along. And you, too, Watson, if you want to go?'

'Try and stop me, sir,' the big Guardsman growled.

51

It was just then that Stirling appeared with a big chart under his arm. He handed it to Lewes who set it up on the easel, which they craned their necks and tried to make out the details, but there was nothing to be seen save that same stretch of North African Coast that they had become all too familiar with over the last few months.

'I hope it ain't gonna be the same old Benghazi handicap,' Smith 175 said, 'I've been up and down this frigging desert half a dozen times since we came out in '40.'

'No, it won't, Smith 175,' Stirling snapped, catching the remark. 'This time we're going up the Blue,' he meant the desert, 'for good.'

'Sorry, sir,' Smith 175 apologized and went red.

'Now then, chaps,' Stirling said, looking hard at Mayne, who had shaved and dabbed talcum powder under his black eye so that he looked a bit more presentable, 'we're away from the Cairo fleshpots, so I can tell you the form because there's no one to blab to out here. General Auchinleck's Eighth Army is going over to the offensive. First he's going to relieve Tobruk here,' he pointed to the besieged port with his pencil. 'Then when he's raised the siege so that his major supply port is open again, he's intending to push on and start forcing Rommel back into

Libya. His final aim is to see Mr Rommel off altogether.'

He paused and let the information sink in for a few moments, then he stopped the excited chatter with, 'Now what role is the SAS going to play in all this? I shall tell you. Intelligence has discovered that the Huns and the Eyeties have five forward airfields between Gazala—here—and Timini—here. General Auchinleck wants them covered before his offensive starts. It will be our job to drop near them and destroy their aircraft an hour before the great offensive starts. It will be our task to drop after nightfall, get in position and one hour before—so that the Huns don't realize until it's too late that this is a major attack—first light. Is that clear?'

'Of course it's clear,' Mayne snarled with some of his old aggressiveness, 'But what's the drill?'

'This. We drop in five separate sticks, one for each enemy airfield—the General has placed five aircraft at our disposal for the drop—each stick will get in position, lie up for the rest of the night and then begin infiltrating the airfield, as I've said, one hour before dawn.'

O'Sullivan felt a sense of growing excitement. Perhaps his old CO, was going to be proved wrong after all. If General Auchinleck was going to place

53

five precious aircraft at the disposal of this new unit, Stirling's force was being taken seriously. Now everything depended upon their carrying out their sabotage mission successfully.

'Once you've done your job you do a very fast bunk,' Stirling was saying. 'You will go to the rendezvous point—here—where the chaps of the Long Range Desert Group will be waiting for you in their vehicles. They will take you to their base at Siwa Oasis—here—and from there back to Kabrit.'

'With fried eggs and bacon and a round of toast for breakfast no doubt,' Mayne said sourly.

'Oh put a sock in it, Paddy,' someone said.

'Well, it's all bloody iffy, ain't it,' Paddy retorted. 'What happens if some of the stick get wounded. Do we leave them behind or what?'

Stirling looked at the Ulsterman coldly. 'Paddy, get this into your thick Irish skull. In the new SAS we are not leaving any of our comrades behind. That's going to be our ground rule number one. In other units you can leave casualties behind, the enemy usually plays the game with the wounded, especially the Hun, but I wonder what they would do to the SAS wounded, especially if we had just blown

54

up one of their airfields?'

'All right,' Mayne persisted undeterred. 'How long is the LRDG going to wait for us? We're five sticks, each coming in a different way. There could be hours difference between the times the sticks reach the rendezvous.'

Stirling was patience itself. 'All right, Paddy, I take your point. I've already talked to the commander of the Long Range Desert Group. I've agreed with him that his people should wait no more than two hours after the agreed rendezvous time. Does that satisfy you?'

Paddy Mayne didn't answer the question. Instead he grumbled, 'It's not that I'm scared of a bit of a barney. It's just that somebody ought to play the Devil's advocate in things like this.'

'All right, then rest your case, Mayne,' Lewes said quietly, 'and let's get on with it.'

Mayne glowered but said nothing.

Stirling took up the briefing again. 'We'll all take a stick. Jock here. You Hastings. Paddy naturally. You Bill...'

O'Sullivan felt like standing up and cheering. Instead he nodded and said 'thank you, sir,' while Stirling continued with the names of the other officers who were going, adding, 'You can pick your own men. Now then, there are only two more things to tell you. One, when we shall be going into action.' He ticked the number off on his finger. 'Next weekend. The Huns usually get pissed in garrison at the weekend. So Auchinleck hopes to take them by surprise.' He grinned and they grinned back at him. 'Two, I think the time has come to show you the design of the regimental badge of the Special Air Service, Jock,' he turned to Lewes, 'will you do the honours?'

'Yes, sir,' Lewes snapped. He opened the box on the trestle table in front of him and brought out a cloth badge. It was in white and blue and featured a flaming sword with wings. Lewes said, 'The badge was designed by our own Sergeant Tait and approved by the CO. We've made a written application to GHQ to have it approved but they turned it down.'

'So, I thought,' Stirling butted in, a grin on his heavy-chinned face, 'bugger it. We're going to have a badge and this is it, authorized or not. And in case you are short-sighted, the regimental motto inscribed upon it is "who dares, wins" '. His grin vanished suddenly to be replaced by a hard look of grim determination. 'And that is exactly what we shall do as long as our regiment exists, we shall dare and we shall *win.*'

The words thrilled O'Sullivan. Suddenly

it came to him. He was a founder member, along with all these grand chaps, of something quite new and different in the British Army. All of its regiments had long traditions and nicknames going back hundreds of years—why there was one Scottish regiment which considered itself so old that its nickname was 'Pontius Pilate's Body guard'. *They* were about to start creating a tradition.

'All right chaps,' Lewes was saying, 'come and collect your badges. Our new berets will be arriving this afternoon.' He grinned. 'The CO wanted them to be white. But I managed to convince him that that wouldn't be a good idea. White is not the best colour for a fighting man.' He shot a mischievous glance at Stirling. Then they were rising to their feet to collect the new badge.

Now time passed quickly as they prepared for their first operation. O'Sullivan was to go with the stick which would be commanded by Mayne, and he realized as the two of them planned their attack, that in addition to being a great brawler, the massive Irishman was a meticulous planner. He was not going to leave anything to chance. As he spelled it out to the younger officer, 'Even the smallest item, Bill, such as the number of salt tablets which we'll take with us can mean disaster in the desert. Up to now we've had quartermasters to do the job for us. Now we've got to do it ourselves.'

Slowly, but with great thoroughness they worked their way through the load each member of the stick would carry, from the amount of the new secret plastic explosive he would take down to the tin of Eno's Fruit Salts which were used to make stale water potable.

In the end the load came to eighty pounds, which Mayne decided was the maximum that each man could carry and still fight. 'We can't go any higher than that, Bill,' he declared, 'but we certainly can't go any lower. It's all right for Stirling to say we'll be picked up by the LRDG, but there's many a slip between the cup and the lip, and I want to be prepared for a long hike home.'

O'Sullivan nodded his agreement. 'You're right, Paddy,' he said. How right the big Irishman was going to be, he little realized at the time.

At dawn one day later when Paddy Mayne was taking on 'any five' in a morning unarmed combat season, throwing the hefty guardsmen around, as if they were lightweights, Lewes appeared and yelled brightly, 'All right, Paddy, save a few of

58

the poor buggers for the Jerries. We're off in an hour. The lorries are coming to fetch us to the airfield.'

'You mean it's tonight!' Paddy exclaimed, wiping the sweat from his baked chest.

'I do,' Lewes beamed at him. 'All right get a bite of breakfast and then get your gear together!'

Spontaneously a great cheer went up from the naked, sweating men and next to a cheering O'Sullivan, Smith 175, who together with Dawson had wangled himself a place in Paddy Mayne's stick, said, 'By crikey, sir, we're off.'

O'Sullivan turned and looked at him, his eyes sparkling with excitement. 'Smith 175, off we are. And y'know I think Colonel Peter was wrong. The world's going to hear a lot of the SAS before this war is over...'

Chapter Six

'Bad news, chaps,' the second pilot of the Bombay bomber yelled, as he came staggering down the fuselage to where the SAS men squatted, backs to the fuselage, 'terrible weather ahead. Met has radioed

59

us.'

They were flying along the coast and had been using its well-designed coastal configurations for navigation. Now they had suddenly vanished and they were flying blind.

'What's the wind speed?' O'Sullivan asked quickly.

'Twenty knots.'

'Holy Jesus, mother of God help and save us,' Paddy Mayne said and crossed himself.

Despite the bad news, O'Sullivan looked at him in astonishment. He'd always taken the Ulsterman to be a Protestant. Now it seems he was a Catholic. He dismissed the thought and said, 'Are you sure? We're not supposed to drop at winds over fifteen knots.'

The second pilot nodded sombrely.

'That's frigging well torn it,' said Smith 175, squatting next to O'Sullivan.

'No, it hasn't,' Mayne said firmly. 'We're going to drop come what may. We can't cock up the regiment's first operational jump.'

'Anyway we're going to go lower and see where we are,' the second pilot said. 'Everything's going for a burton this bloody night.' He turned and staggered back up to the cockpit.

Five minutes later they heard what

60

seemed the beak of some gigantic bird rapping on the metal fuselage. For a moment they were puzzled, but when suddenly a great hole was ripped in the metal and a blast of icy air blew in, they knew what it was. *'Flak!'* O'Sullivan yelled.

In that same moment the big bomber staggered as if it had run into a wall. For an instant they thought they were going to plunge straight into the desert below. But, face red with the effort, muscles straining through the thin material of his flying suit, the pilot managed to keep the Bombay in the air.

'We've been hit in the port engine,' the co-pilot yelled over his shoulder. 'But we're holding, sir.'

Now shells seemed to be exploding around them everywhere. An angry red tracer zipped lethally through the darkness.

'Bugger this for a lark!' Mayne cried, rising to his feet and putting on his jumping helmet. 'We're getting out of here while we're still in once piece. Prepare to jump.'

The men needed no urging. Hurriedly they hooked up and lined up behind Mayne and O'Sullivan.

'But we can't find the DZ,' the second pilot objected.

'We'll make our own,' Mayne yelled

back. Next moment he had launched himself out into space. In an instant he had disappeared into the inky darkness.

O'Sullivan took a deep breath and jumped too. Instantly the terrible wind grabbed him. He was swung the length of the damaged plane, thrust through lines of white tracer like glowing golf balls. A sharp crack and a tug under his armpits. The chute had opened. Desperately he fought the shroud lines, praying that the wind wouldn't get inside the canopy. It didn't. Seconds later he hit the ground—hard. But the ordeal wasn't over yet.

Abruptly he found himself being dragged across the surface like a kite. He yelped as he hit a rock and then another. Desperately he fought to free himself. All around the sandstorm raged. Finally he succeeded in releasing the harness. For a moment he just lay there, fighting for breath, for the wind seemed to snatch the very air out of his lungs.

Then—cautiously—he raised himself. He had not broken anything. But it was damnably difficult to stand upright, with the wind buffeting his body. But he knew he had to keep on his feet and find the others. He took out his torch and started flashing the recognition signal, turning a circle as he did so.

At first there was nothing. Then through

the flying sand, he caught a sudden winking light to his right. Bent double and gasping like an asthmatic in the throes of an attack, he fought his way over to where the light was flashing. 'Smith 175,' he gasped with relief 'it's you!'

'Yes, sir, turned up like the proverbial bad penny, but where's the rest of the mob, sir?' Smith yelled.

'Well, we've just got to go and find 'em. Come on.'

It took two hours, with lots of flashing torches and shouting against the howling of the storm, to find the rest, including Mayne, who was the last to link up with the stick. He was in a foul temper and there was still blood trickling down the side of his craggy face from a gash in his forehead. 'What a cock-up!' he cried. 'God knows what happened to the others! Still no matter, I've found the Eyetie field.'

'Good show!' O'Sullivan said.

'Not so bloody good show,' Paddy Mayne growled angrily. 'We've still not found the container with our heavy weapons and most of the bombs. Still we'll have to do the job with what we've got. Come on.' Without waiting to see if they were following, he started to stride away fighting the wind with all that brutal strength of his.

Ten minutes later they reached the perimeter wire of their objective and in lulls in the storm, they could catch glimpses of the landing lights lining the field's flare path. 'All right,' Mayne snarled, 'don't stand there like a fart in a trance, Smith 175. You've got the wire cutters. Use 'em!'

Hurriedly the big Guardsman bent and started snipping through the wire, while the others crouched in a tense semicircle, weapons at the ready, peering through the flying sand for any sign of the enemy.

'Ready, sir,' Smith gasped after a few minutes.

'All right,' Mayne ordered. 'As soon as we get to the hangars, spread out and deal with your planes. Come on.'

Hastily they slipped through the hole in the wire, telling themselves that the sandstorm was now proving their ally; it was giving the protection they needed from prowling sentries. On a night like this they would be sticking close to the cover of the airfield's buildings.

They reached the flare path and, keeping away from the faint red light cast by the landing lights, they started to follow it to the taxi area where the first of the Italian planes probably would be lined up for an emergency take-off. It would be those planes that Auchinleck would want knocked out first.

Five minutes passed. Still the storm raged. It was something the intruders were thankful for. Then the Italians were decidedly careless about their blackout and they glimpsed chinks of light from many of the huts that they passed. They were all obviously occupied by enemy soldiers.

'Fiat fighters,' Mayne hissed and held up his hand for them to stop.

'Where?' O'Sullivan asked.

'Over there to the right,' Mayne whispered back. 'Come on let's get them.'

Hurriedly the SAS men spread out as they had trained to do, without orders. Each man took a separate plane, clamped a lump of plastic explosive on the engine cowling and thrust home the time pencil which would detonate the new secret explosive. Timed to go off in fifteen minutes, it meant they had that amount of time to carry out further sabotage.

They moved, leaving ten of the sleek Italian fighters timed to disintegrate in a quarter of an hour.

Then Smith 175 spotted the fuel dump. A hundred square yards of high octane aviation fuel, kept in great steel barrels.

'Luvverly grub,' Mayne chortled happily. 'Wait till this little lot goes up. Burn the whole bloody place down. Come on new, gildly. Let's get to it.'

They needed no urging. They all knew that time was running out for them. There were ten minutes left before the time pencils exploded the plastic; then all hell would break loose with the wind buffeting them like blows from a giant fist, the little group of saboteurs slipped from barrel to barrel setting their charges, so that the whole dump was crisscrossed with plastic explosive and they had none of the explosives, which stank of almonds and had given them all headaches from its fumes, left.

Paddy Mayne flashed a quick look at the green-glowing dial of his wrist-watch. 'Five minutes left. Come on, lads, let's beat—'

'*Alt, Che é la?*' an anxious voice demanded in Italian.

'Christ,' Dawson exclaimed, 'an Eyetie.'

Suddenly a little man emerged from the whirling gloom, some kind of submachine-gun held against his side.

'He's going to fire!' O'Sullivan yelled in alarm in the same instant that Mayne threw himself forward in one of those celebrated tackles of his which had made him the darling of the spectators before the war.

The Italian screamed and in the same moment that he went reeling backwards, he pressed the trigger of his machine pistol. Tracer went winging into the night sky in

66

a stream of burning white.

Mayne punched him in the face. He felt the Italian's nose burst under the impact of his hamlike fist. Hot blood spurted all over his hand. Then he was up, yelling, 'All right, lads back to the perimeter. The balloon's gonna go up in half a mo.'

Mayne was right. Suddenly lights were flashing everywhere. There were cries, shouts, orders. Someone shrilled a whistle. A klaxon started to whine dolefully. Searchlights flicked on, icy fingers of light attempted to see through the sandstorm and they were running for all they were worth for the wire and the desert beyond.

'La!' Someone yelled urgently.

'They've spotted us,' O'Sullivan cried, arms working back and forth like pistons, as he fled with the others.

A searchlight started to edge towards the fugitives, its icy white beam searching the ground. O'Sullivan stopped for a moment. He pressed the trigger of his Tommy gun. There was a scream, a tinkle of broken glass and the light went out abruptly.

'Good for you, Bill,' Mayne panted. 'Come on, lads, we're almost there now.'

Now they could see the perimeter wire vaguely. As they ran, Smith 175 prepared his wire cutters. They came to a halt, chests heaving frantically, the beads of

67

sweat streaming down their tense anxious faces.

Smith flung himself down, while the others faced outwards, weapons at the ready. He started to snip the wires frantically, knowing that if they were caught now, they were sitting ducks. Strand after strand broke. He judged he had cut enough. With his bare hands he forced the wires outwards, feeling the barbs cut cruelly into his palms. He bit his bottom lip till the blood came, to stop himself from crying out. Then he'd done it, a gap big enough for a man to crawl through. 'Ready, sir,' he said thickly.

'One by one,' Mayne ordered glaring into the night, as if he were daring any Italian attempting to stop them.

Frantically they squirmed their way through the gap till all of them were outside the perimeter. 'What now, Paddy?' O'Sullivan asked. 'The RZ with the LRDG?'

Mayne shook his head. 'Look at that,' he snorted. On the desert road some two hundred yards away, a huge convoy with dimmed headlights was heading east. 'Not a chance of getting through that without being caught, Bill. I think the whole op has been a cock-up.'

'What'll we do then?' O'Sullivan asked a little helplessly.

Mayne gave him a slap across the shoulder that nearly knocked him off his feet. '*Nil desperandum,* old boy,' he said heartily. 'We'll stick to the coast till we meet our own chaps. We're going to hoof it...'

One minute later they had vanished into the night. The long march home had commenced.

Chapter Seven

'It's a damn poor show, Stirling,' the major of the Long Range Desert Group agreed as they sat together in the big Dodge, as they bounced their way across the desert. 'Awfully bad luck, indeed.'

David Stirling nodded his head glumly, noting that the sand was quite firm on the old camel route, the Trig El Abd, which led to to LRDG's base at the oasis. 'Two of my sticks, including Paddy Mayne's, are completely missing and the other three took a bad beating. I'd say we've lost over a half of our strength.'

'Did you have any success?' the other officer asked, as to the east the morning flickered a silent pink, which indicated the barrage had started. Auchinleck's great offensive had commenced.

'Not that I know of. I certainly didn't. By the time my stick got within sight of the objective, the enemy had been alerted.' He frowned. 'We came under a hellish volume of fire. I lost two chaps, first-rate men at that, and I was forced to retire in the end, with nothing to show for it.'

'Well, you were just unlucky, Stirling. That sandstorm did it I suppose.'

He turned and looked at the dejected, unshaven Guards officer. 'If I may make a suggestion, Stirling?'

'Yes, please go ahead.' Stirling answered without much apparent interest.

'I would forego the parachuting business. It's too dicey in the desert with these sudden sandstorms and all the thermals we get from the sudden changes in temperature. The next time, I'd use the same means we do—long range vehicles. They're safer.'

'If there is a next time,' Stirling said gloomily. 'My enemies at GHQ will be rubbing their hands with glee once they hear our first op was a total failure. They'll try to get the ear of the general and once they do, he'll close us down.'

'Don't be so downhearted, Stirling,' the other officer chided him, as on the horizon they could see the first patch of green which indicated that they were approaching the oasis-base of the LRDG. 'Keep out of sight for a while.'

Stirling perked up. 'How do you mean?'

'Well, you don't have to go back to Kabrit, do you?'

'No, I don't suppose so. But where will I go?'

'Stay with us. You can ask the CO if it's all right. We've got plenty of grub etc, and the only contact we've got with Cairo is by radio. As long as we do our job—reconnaissance of enemy movements and report our findings back to GHQ, the brass-hats leave us strictly in peace.'

Stirling sucked his front teeth as he thought over the suggestion. He knew he needed to redeem the reputation of the new SAS if his creation was going to survive. But first his men needed rest and reorganization. After that he would have to pull off some coup that would impress Auchinleck. 'Let me ask you a quick question. If parachuting is out for us, do you think your mob could deliver us where we needed to be for a raid?'

'As I've just said,' the other officer replied, 'our job is reconnaissance. But if your plans don't clash with our job, I don't see why the CO would object to delivering you to your objective, Stirling. Think it over.'

Stirling did. As the little convoy rolled

71

through the desert towards Siwa Oasis, he told himself he'd follow the LRDG man's advice. He'd stay with them while he reorganized. The LRDG would be ideal for his next raid. Naturally it would take longer than by plane to infiltrate—there were two hundred miles of desert to be covered to the coast—but the LRDG people were masters of desert reconnaissance, with impeccable navigational skills. They'd get him to his objective all right, he was quite sure of that.

That night as they huddled in their bedrolls under a star-studded velvet sky, Stirling was unable to sleep; he was thinking too hard. He lay under his blankets, hands propped under his head, looking at the harsh silver of the stars, which seemed so close that he felt he could reach out and grab one. All around him he could hear the eerie singing of the sand. Millions of sand grains which contracted at night due to the sudden cold and were now moving, rubbing against one another, giving off a strange haunting music.

If the LRDG's CO would back him, he had decided, he would obtain reinforcements and fresh weapons somehow. From the Oasis base the reformed SAS would strike as soon as it was ready and before GHQ cottoned on to the fact that the survivors had not returned to Kabrit. After all, as of yet nobody but the men snoring all around him knew of the failure of the raid on the five airfields. Thus it would be possible to stage another raid before some brass hat at GHQ ordered the SAS to be disbanded.

Stirling felt a return of his old confidence, that belief in himself and the unit he had created.

Hadn't he told 'the Auk', as the commanding general was nicknamed—behind his back: 'Sir, some of our staff are thinking in terms of trench warfare. Mass action by thousands of men, all arranged according to timetables, startlines and all the rest of that staff college stuff. But, in my opinion, sir, a handful of tough, well-trained men, who play rough and play to win, can do more damage than a whole battalion—perhaps even a brigade—of conventional infantry.'

He still believed that. But he knew he had to prove it to the staff wallahs. But how? It wouldn't be by knocking out a few aircraft or blowing up an enemy supply dump. It had to be something more spectacular than that. *But what?*

In the end he drifted off into a troubled sleep, his problem still not solved...

'Your Captain Lewes, I'm afraid,' Major Steele of the LRDG, welcomed the survivors the next morning with the bad news, 'is dead, one of our patrols which

73

came in earlier found his body. We couldn't bring the body back because they had just bumped into a party of Eyeties and there was quite a party going on. In short my chaps did a bunk.' The bronzed LRDG man with his Arab headdress, which all of them wore, looked unhappy for a moment or two. 'Fortunes of war, I suppose. Come on and have cup of tea.'

Buried in thought Stirling accompanied him to the blazing petrol-tin fire, over which a soldier was boiling the water for the usual dawn brew-up. 'Sarnt-major's char,' the soldier said cheerfully and started pouring a full tin of Carnation Evaporated Milk into the tea dixie. 'Can stand a spoon upright in it.'

'Anything on my chap Mayne?' Stirling asked.

Major Steele shook his head. 'Not a sausage. Of course, since the balloon went up yesterday morning, everything's been totally topsy-turvy.'

'Here's yer char, sir,' the cheerful private thrust a battered enamel mug at a miserable Stirling.

He accepted it gratefully and Steele said, 'Fancy a little whisky in it. I know the sun's a long way from being over the yard-arm, but it does take out the damn cold.' He pulled out a silver flask and poured a little of its contents into Stirling's mug.

Stirling took a drink of the scalding hot brew and felt a little better. 'Can you stand me and my chaps here for a few days till we get ourselves sorted out, major?' he asked. 'I'd like to have another crack at the enemy—and this is pretty close to them.'

'Naturally, old chap,' Steele agreed. 'Indeed there is some sort of op being planned, which will involve us and the 11th Scottish Commando. Don't know much about it yet. Though they say it's going to be pretty hairy. We could use some extra muscle. Your chaps would fit in very nicely, I should imagine.'

Stirling's face lit up. 'An op!' he exclaimed. 'When?'

'Don't know exactly, but it's all very dependent on how the current offensive against Rommel goes. If it doesn't work out as the Auk plans, so I'm told, then the op goes ahead. All very puzzling, what, Stirling?'

'Yes, it is. All the same it's a chance for us to redeem ourselves before it is too late.' He took another drink of the scalding tea, face now thoughtful. 'I wonder what it is?'

The LRDG major finished his tea and said, rising to his feet, 'Got to take a spade for a walk. The old guts are churning. Suppose I've got the bloody gippo tummy again. It's all these damned flies.' He grabbed a handful of 'Army Form Blank', the khaki-coloured army lavatory paper, and unclipped a spade from the side of the Dodge. Then he set off. Just as he breasted the dune, he shouted over his shoulder, 'And by the way, rumour has it that this particular op, if it comes off, has been planned by the jolly old PM—Churchill—himself.' Then he was gone, leaving Stirling squatting there in front of the blue-burning petrol fire, his face a mixture of excitement and bewilderment, as he wondered what Winston Churchill could have to do with an operation at such a low level...

The next few days passed swiftly. While Stirling attempted to rally and rearm his somewhat demoralized little force, the patrol of the LRDG ranged far and wide on the flanks of the *Afrikakorps,* as the Eighth Army strove valiantly to reach Tobruk. But the news wasn't good.

When the patrols returned to the oasis, they brought with them increasingly gloomy forecasts that the steam was running out of the British offensive. The German resistance was stiffening all the while and the offensive was slowing down significantly.

'We're battering ourselves bloody against the Hun,' Major Steele, his face weary and hollow, told Stirling two days later. 'Our tanks are no match for the Jerry Mark IVs and those bloody great 88 millimetre cannons of theirs. Yesterday I saw a whole regiment—I think it was the 8th Irish Hussars—being brewed up by a handful of Mark IVs supported by 88s. Their guns simply outrange ours by a thousand yards or more.' And he swallowed his whisky in bitter anger.

Two more days passed and it was clear from the signals coming in from GHQ that the offensive was slowing down. Casualties were heavy and some of the armoured regiments were down to a handful of tanks.

More and more the staff officers at GHQ were demanding information on how fast the Germans were withdrawing and as Major Steele told Stirling, 'They're in for a bloody disappointment. The Hun is digging his bloody heels in. The Eyeties are still retreating. Anyway Rommel is simply using them as cannonfodder, while he conserves the *Afrikakorps*.' He shook his head. 'Personally I think we've had it. Soon the Eighth Army will be galloping the Benghazi Handicap once more.' He meant retreating.

Then, the same day that the men at the oasis heard from a BBC broadcast that the offensive was being halted 'temporarily'

77

to enable 'the 8th Army to tidy up its flanks and its supply columns to catch up with it'—'the usual bloody lies,' someone commented bitterly, as they grouped round the wireless—they received a signal that 'Plan R is to be put into operation,' it stated briefly. 'Report to GHQ by zero eight hundred hours, Friday.' It was signed 'Auchinleck.'

Steele handed the message to Stirling and when he had read it, he said, 'Stirling, I think this is the chance you and your SAS chaps have been waiting for. You'd better come with me. Now let's get cracking. Pack your best bib-and-tucker for GHQ. We've got a long journey in front of us...'

Chapter Eight

They had been marching for days now. Mostly they had marched at night and laid up in the desert during the daylight hours. By now they were exhausted and were existing on hard tack and at the most half a bottle of water per day. But they were not prepared to give in and surrender, for they were slowly approaching the front. Now they could see the flame and the great columns of black smoke rising into the sky which indicated yet another tank had been brewed up.

There were Germans and Italians everywhere. The latter seemed to be retreating while the Germans were still going up, great columns of tanks and infantry in trucks. Once they had been caught by surprise when a convoy of Italian soldiers pulled up close to them. But Mayne reacted correctly right away. 'Sing...sing any bloody thing,' he ordered. 'The Jerries always bloody well sing.'

And so dressed only in their khaki shorts and shirts, which was the same uniform worn by the *Afrikakorps,* they marched past the Italians, lathered in a sweat of apprehension, but lustily singing, 'Now this is number one, and I've got 'er on the run, roll me over in the clover, roll me over and do it agen...'

On the afternoon of the fourth day of their escape, they started to encounter the German rear line positions, gun parks, petrol depots and the like and Mayne decided it was time to plan getting through the German front line.

He ordered his little command to move into the shade of a red cliff not far from the sea. There they crouched in the growing darkness while the guns thundered to their front, eating the tiny sweet dates they had found in the palms and taking careful sips of their remaining water. 'It's got to be tonight,' Mayne declared staring around at their drawn, exhausted faces in the gloom. 'We daren't be caught out in the open in daylight. Too damned dangerous.' He wet his parched cracked lips and told himself he'd give a fortune for a pint of Guiness.

'We'll have to keep well away from the coastal road,' O'Sullivan suggested. 'Too full of Jerry transport.'

'Yes, you're right,' Mayne agreed. 'We'll go in on this left flank close to the sea. That will be the Jerries' static area, where they'll be dug in. The right flank'll be fluid. There we run the risk of bumping into their mobile units.'

'What about this cliff or hill, sir?' Smith 175 suggested. 'If they've got anything up there it'll probably be an OP at the most,' he meant an observation post, ' 'cos I bet you'll get a good view from up there.'

Mayne sucked his teeth thoughtfully, 'Perhaps you're right, Smith 175. Up there at least we'd get a picture of what is going on at the front and make out the Hun dispositions from their gun flashes and the like.' He rose and stared at the cliff. 'Not too steep, but there's devil of a lot of camel thorn on its face,' he mused aloud.

'Better a few scratches, sir,' Guardsman Dawson said, 'than a frigging Jerry bayonet up yer jacksey.'

That made them laugh and again O'Sullivan was glad that the two Guardsmen had 'deserted' to join this new unit. He said, 'What do you think, Paddy? When?'

'Give it half an hour until it's properly dark, Bill,' Mayne answered. 'There'll be a half moon tonight so we'll have enough light, but not too bloody much.' He raised his voice. 'Search yer packs. If you've got a spare pair of socks, use them as gloves. If you've got a face cloth, see if you can tie it around yer knees. Those bloody camel thorns hurt. I know—I've had them stuck in me.'

At ten o'clock precisely that night they set off, each man knowing that they had—at the most—eight hours to get through the German frontline before daylight came. Mayne paused at the base of red cliff. 'Looks a bad bugger, Bill,' he said and then he reached upwards. The climb had commenced.

Spread out in twos, the others followed the two officers in the lead as they started to pull their way upwards, dodging the vicious camel thorn the best they could. Within minutes they were lathered with sweat despite the coldness of the night. Foot by foot they worked their way upwards, letting off stifled yelps when they encountered those cruel thorns which

81

ripped and tore at their flesh.

It was murderous going. Digging their toes into the sandy rock of the cliff, clinging on till the ends of their fingers were numb with pain, they edged their way upwards in grim determination. Once O'Sullivan, panting like an old man, hung perilously by his hands, unable to move for the thorns which had fastened themselves on his ripped, torn shorts. Desperately, face dripping with sweat, he twisted and turned to free himself from the barbs which had dug deep into his flesh. As one gave way, another lashed across his face tearing the flesh cruelly in a dozen spots. He stifled a cry of pain, as blood ran into his mouth, and went on.

Behind him he could hear Dawson and Smith 175 making a better go of it. They were following the trail he was blazing, finding the way cleared of the worst obstacles at the expense of his poor torn, bleeding body. But worn as he was, he felt a sense of pride when he heard Smith 175 gasp 'Young Mr O'Sullivan is a fine gent. He's taking a lot o' bleeding stick on our account.'

O'Sullivan pushed on. He placed his foot in a hole in the rock and reached his hand up to the sharp end of a flattish rock just above his head. The foothole gave way suddenly. His hand slipped and the rock ripped off a fingernail. An electric wave of almost unbearable pain shot through his body. He swung his face into the dirt and bit off some of it to stifle his cry of agony.

Then he'd made it. Before him he saw the clearly defined edge of the cliff outlined against the deep purple of the night sky. Frantically he clawed his way over the edge to collapse on the ground, panting heavily, the blood dribbling from a myriad cuts all over his poor tortured body.

Mayne, followed a few moments later by the others, dropped next to him and together they all stared to their front, trying to penetrate the inky gloom.

'At three o'clock, sir,' Smith 175, who had the sharpest eyes of them all, whispered tensely. 'Looks like a little camp o' tents.'

'Got it,' Mayne said. 'Yes, you're right. I count half a dozen of 'em.' He rose cautiously and doubled a fist like a small steam shovel. 'On yer feet,' he ordered.

He waited till they had risen before ordering again, 'You know unarmed combat the lot of you. So if we run into trouble, don't use your weapons unless you have to. Knock the buggers out with yer hands. Come on.'

Cautiously, noiselessly, they stole forward in an extended line, heading for the little camp of tents in the saucerlike depression at the top of the cliff.

Mayne halted when they were a dozen yards away from the first tent. 'Looks like they've got a sentry. There's a chap sitting on a chair outside the tent.'

Dawson cocked his head to one side. 'Yer, and he's having a drop of shut-eye, sir. I can hear the Jerry sod snoring.'

'All to the good,' Mayne hissed. 'Come on.'

'Shall I see him off, sir?' Dawson asked softly.

'All right. Off you go,' Mayne agreed.

Dawson doubled forward noiselessly, body crouched low. As he did so something silver sparkled in his hand in the spectral light of the half-moon. O'Sullivan caught his breath. The big Guardsman was going to knife the sleeping sentry.

Suddenly Dawson stumbled and almost fell. He caught himself in time. But the damage had been done. Slowly, almost stupidly, the sentry opened his eyes. His face, seen in that silver light, registered surprise, then shock. He opened his mouth, he was about to yell. Dawson dived forward. One big hand went round the German's mouth stifling the cry of alarm. Next moment Dawson slid his knife into the man's ribs as the chair flew backwards.

There was a stifled moan. The listeners could hear a terrible sucking noise as

Dawson thrust home the knife once more and then again. An instant later he rose to his feet and waved at them.

'Come on,' Mayne hissed.

They needed no urging. They surged forward, crouched low, ready for trouble.

They found it soon enough. From one of the tents there came a cry of alarm.

'Sod it,' Smith 175 hissed. 'We've bin rumbled.'

A half-naked man came hopping out of the tent, trying to pull on his right boot. O'Sullivan fired instinctively. For a moment the man looked at the red stain in his white undershirt stupidly as if he couldn't comprehend how it got there. Then he pitched face forward to the ground.

The single shot signalled the alarm. There were cries, yells of rage and orders being yelled angrily. Men started to pour from the tents, milling around in confusion.

Now the SAS troopers knew they would have to fight for their lives. Without being ordered they opened fire. The Germans scattered in wild confusion leaving two of their numbers sprawled out in the sand in the grotesque extravagant postures of those violently donc to death.

Spread out in a rough line firing from the hip as they did so, the fugitives pushed their way through the camp. Here and there the Germans tried to put up some resistance, but they had been caught by surprise and were, for the most part, without their weapons. O'Sullivan, in the lead, snapped off aimed shots to left and right, killing and wounding with cold, calculating anger.

A gigantic German, armed with a meat cleaver, came running round from behind one of the tents, cursing furiously. O'Sullivan was caught by surprise. Then he remembered the danger he was in. He pressed the trigger of his .38. Nothing happened!

The big German yelled in triumph. He raised the cleaver and was just about to crash it down on O'Sullivan's bare head when Dawson reacted faster. 'None of that there here!' he cried and threw his knife. The German screamed shrilly, high and hysterical like a woman. With trembling fingers he tried to pluck the knife from his big chest, to no avail. Next moment he pitched to the ground, dead before he hit the sand.

'Thank you, Dawson,' O'Sullivan yelled over his shoulder. 'You saved my bacon that time.' And then they were through the camp, leaving behind them dead and dying Germans, running for the darkness of the plain below.

Chapter Nine

It was furnace hot, although it was only half an hour after dawn. They had failed to get through in the hours of darkness; now the survivors of Mayne's stick slogged on through the burning heat. Not a breath of air stirred. Now and again they stopped and, shading their eyes, stared at the sun. It was like a dirty brown coin seen at the bottom of a village pond. And all of them knew what that meant. They were in for another sandstorm.

Mayne, wiping the sweat off his bronzed face and swatting at the flies which buzzed around them everywhere, said, 'It might be a blessing in disguise, lads. It could give us the cover we need if we're going to get through to our own lines.'

O'Sullivan didn't say it aloud, but thought that it could also present a new danger. In the midst of a raging sandstorm they might well stumble into a German position.

It was an hour later when the sandstorm caught them. They had just circled a German gun site, the enemy gunners too busy firing a barrage to notice them, when it started. Abruptly the sun vanished and the sky darkened ominously. The first gust of wind hit them like a physical blow. They were stopped in their tracks, gasping and panting for air.

'This is it,' Mayne roared, as day seemed to turn into night. 'Hold on to the belt of bloke in front of you. I'll take the lead. You bring up the rear, Bill.'

They carried out his orders the best they could. Bent double almost, they staggered forward, groping through the whirling sand like old blind men. The wind rose in fury, shrieking and wailing like banshees. In an instant they were gasping for breath in that burning sand, which struck their faces like a wall of hot stilettos. They opened their mouths to howl with pain. But wind snatched the cries from their gaping, gasping mouths.

Breathing became very difficult. The howling hellish fog of sand threatened to choke them. Above their heads the ululating threnody rose to an ever louder fury. The hot wind had travelled a thousand miles across the burning Sahara to seize its victims. Now it lashed and thrashed their bodies as if determined not to let them escape. Time and time again it smashed them with what seemed a gigantic fist. O'Sullivan felt more than once that he was going to be blown off his feet and carried away helplessly across the desert floor.

Once in a momentary pause, O'Sullivan peered through his sand-caked desert goggles and thought, for a fleeting second, that he saw something darker than the yellow sand. But before he was able to identify it, the wind descended upon them once more with renewed fury. It wailed and howled madly, as if determined that these puny mortals should be wiped off the face of the earth for having had the temerity to venture into its burning kingdom.

Then almost as suddenly as it had begun, it was over. The savage frightening roar was replaced by a softer, ever-decreasing dirge. Then it was gone altogether. Silence, heavy and awesome, fell over the desert.

Mayne gave a sigh of relief and started patting the caked sand off his shirt. Others took off their sand goggles and rubbed their faces, running their tongues over their parched lips so that the lips appeared a blood-red against the mask of sand.

It was Smith 175 who spotted the danger first. 'Christ, sir!' he exclaimed excitedly, 'there's a tank—a Jerry tank just over there.'

'What!' O'Sullivan snapped. He turned and looked in the direction that Smith was pointing. 'My God, you're right!'

Only yards away there was a Mark III,

the iron cross clearly visible on its side, its engine still running—they could hear it in the sudden stillness—but with its turret buttoned down.

'Come on, he hissed, reacting swiftly, 'let's get the bastard before they open the hatch and spot us.'

Hurriedly they ran to the tank, nerves racing electrically, tensing expectantly for the first burst of machine gun fire from the turret when the Germans spotted them.

For a moment as they reached the tank, they were at a loss about what to do. How were they going to penetrate the Mark III's armour? Then O'Sullivan had an idea. 'Anyone still got a grenade?' he whispered urgently, knowing that in a minute the tank crew inside would begin to stir.

'Yes, me sir,' Dawson said.

'Give it to me.'

Hastily O'Sullivan took the egg-shaped grenade, sprang on the tank, pulled out the pin and rolled the deadly little egg down the barrel of the Mark III's cannon. In that same instant, he dived over the side. He hit the sand. All around him the others crouched, arms protecting their faces.

There was a muffled cry of anger from within the tank. The crew had obviously heard the grenade rattle down the barrel. There was a rusty squeak. Someone was opening the hatch. He never made it.

The grenade exploded. There was a shrill scream. A thin wedge of grey smoke drifted from the partly opened hatch. Next moment it was flung open altogether and a black-faced crewman emerged, only to slump half way out, dead or unconscious.

Mayne didn't waste any time. 'Come on, let's winkle the sods out. That's our wheels—or tracks.' He laughed crazily. 'We're going to ride the rest of the sodding way in style. I'm sick of marching.'

Five minutes later with a scared *Afrikakorps* driver at the controls of the battered tank, they were rolling eastwards, guzzling the German crew's water ration and swallowing great chunks of spicy salami. Behind them on the blackened sand they left the crew, dead or unconscious. 'Now this is what I call style,' Smith 175 chortled, as he stood next to O'Sullivan in the blackened turret, puffing at a captured cigar. 'I swear I'll never frigging well walk agen...'

The solid white armour-piercing shell came whizzing across the desert to meet them. It missed by a few feet and slammed into the sand behind them. The desert erupted into a whirling spout of earth and sand. Down in his compartment the German driver slammed on the brakes and cried over the intercom. *'Die schiessen, Herr Leutenant!...Bitte was soll ich machen?'*

O'Sullivan didn't understand much German, but he didn't need to. Another shell fired from the anti-tank gun to their right told him all he need to know. 'We've reached British lines,' he yelled urgently, as a heavy machine gun started to add its fire to that of the anti-tank, 'bale out, lads...And put your hands above your heads. They think we're Jerries...'

They scrambled madly out of the still moving tank and dropped into the sand, as the German driver below continued to drive towards the British front. Not for long, though. There was the great hollow boom of metal striking metal. The Mark III came to an abrupt stop. It reared up on its back boogies like a wild horse being put to the saddle for the first time. Next moment it slammed down again and burst into flame. The driver didn't get out.

'Poor sod,' Smith 175 said unfeelingly, as they filed towards the British lines hands held well up in the air, 'he should have learned English.'

'We have been told to look out for you—er—SAS people,' the brigade intelligence officer said, as O'Sullivan and Mayne sat in his tent drinking whisky and soda. Up front the guns—German ones now—thundered again and a weary but happy O'Sullivan told himself that the

British offensive had come to a halt. Soon the Germans would be doing the attacking. Then 'the Benghazi Handicap', as Smith 175 had called it, would commence and the Eighth Army would be retreating yet again. He shook his head and told himself that the war in the desert seemed to be going on for ever. Nobody appeared able to win it.

'In fact,' the Intelligence Major was saying, 'we've been ordered to dispatch you to Cairo immediately, if and when you turned up.'

Mayne whistled softly. 'Cairo!' he exclaimed. 'The jolly old fleshpots again.'

The Major looked at Mayne's dirty, unshaven, tough face and told himself he wouldn't like to meet the hulking Irishman on a dark night. He shook his head. ' 'Fraid you won't have much time for the fleshpots, Mayne. There's a big op on—and you lot—the—er—SAS... I still can't get used to those initials...'

'They'll grow on you, sir,' Mayne said cheerfully and took another tremendous swig at his whisky.

'I'm sure they will,' the other officer answered, as the walls of the tent flapped in and out with the blast of the British counter-barrage. Outside tanks were rumbling by. Obviously the Germans were beginning a local counter-attack. 'Anyway,' the Intelligence man raised his voice above the racket, 'you chaps are needed urgently for this new op.'

'What is it?' O'Sullivan asked. 'Can you give us a clue sir?'

' 'Fraid I can't. All very hush-hush and top level. The CG'—he meant Auchinleck—'is involved. All I can tell you is that you are to be whipped off to Cairo as soon as possible.'

'To whom do we report, sir?' Mayne asked, draining his glass and looking at the bottle of whisky on the trestle table longingly.

The Major ignored the look. If things went the way he thought they would this day, he'd need all the whisky he could find. He was not going to waste any on greedy Irishmen. 'You're to go to GHQ and there you'll report to the HQ of the 11th Scottish Commando.'

'*What?*' Mayne exploded, half rising from his stool. 'What did you say, sir?'

The Major looked at him puzzled. 'To the HQ of the 11th Scottish Commando, in particular to a Lieutenant Colonel Keyes.' He saw the look on the big Irishman's tough face and added, 'Why, do you know him?'

'Do I know him,' Mayne echoed through gritted teeth.

Next to him, O'Sullivan looked at

Paddy's grim face and remembered when he had first met Paddy Mayne at the bar of Shepheard's, escorted by two armed officers and under open arrest for having struck Keyes and having chased him out of the mess with a naked bayonet.

'Have you any idea why we are involved?' O'Sullivan began, but the rest of his question was drowned by the rattle of a heavy machine gun close by and an angry voice crying, 'The sods have broken through...we're pulling back, lads!'

The Intelligence officer grabbed for his helmet and then as an afterthought for the bottle of whisky on the trestle, 'I think, gentlemen, the time for talking is over. I rather gather that we'll soon be doing a bunk. Come on, quick!'

O'Sullivan shook his head. Rommel, the Desert Fox, had done it again. And then he, too, was running with the rest, while behind them the British front broke and the panzers started to stream through.

PART TWO

Failure Of A Mission

'When you burst into a hut full of enemy soldiers, you must remember the drill evolved for such occasions. Shoot the first person who makes a move, hostile or otherwise. His brain has recovered from the shock of seeing you there with a gun. He has started to think and therefore he is dangerous. You must then shoot the person nearest to you because he is in the best position to cause you embarrassment. Then deal with the rest as you think fit.'

The Sayings of Paddy Mayne

Chapter One

'There's one hell of a flap going on!' Stirling exclaimed as they left the native suburbs of Cairo, with the half-starved dogs, beggars crying out for *bakeesh* and barefoot boys blinded with *bilharzia,* and entered the European quarter.

Everywhere Europeans were lugging heavy suitcases down to their cars. Chauffeurs were hooting their horns impatiently. Children, many of them crying, were being comforted or scolded by their harassed mothers and nannies, as they prepared to leave for the safety of Palestine. Staff officers were ushering their elegant wives or mistresses into Daimlers to take them to the main station, where hundreds were waiting impatiently in the blazing sun, jeered at by the Egyptians, who knew they were fleeing before Rommel came.

'Bloody lily-livered civvies,' Mayne sneered moodily, as their jeep wound its way in and out of the panic-stricken mob. 'Thrown in the bloody towel already. No guts.'

O'Sullivan grinned. No one could accuse the big Irishman of not having guts. He'd probably volunteer to fight the *Afrikakorps* single-handed if asked. All the same he could see that Paddy was worried at the thought he'd be meeting his old CO very soon; and Stirling had already warned him, 'Now Paddy, I want you to be on your best behaviour. Remember we're not being paid to fight *each other*. We're being paid to fight old Jerry. Put that in your pipe and smoke it.' There had been no response from Mayne.

Smith 175 at the wheel of their jeep halted to let a convoy of Australians heading for the front go by. As usual with the Australians they were drunk, and yelling insults to both the civilians and Egyptians alike. They knew their lives 'up the blue' were going to be short and brutal. They didn't care. When they saw the three officers in the jeep, they cried, 'Hello there, Pommies! Hope yer've got yer running shoes, So yer can take off faster.'

Mayne flushed red and half rose to his feet, clenching his massive fists, 'Why you cheeky Aussie buggers. I've half a mind to—'

'Sit down for God's sake,' Stirling ordered, placing a big hand on Mayne's shoulder in the very same instant that an Egyptian in a shabby European suit crossed over to the stationary jeep. He lifted up a cigarette and said in broken English, 'You got fire for cigarette. English gentleman?'

'What the devil?' O'Sullivan began, then he realized that the fat little civilian was staring hard at his badge. He wasn't one bit interested in obtaining a light. 'Hey, what's your game?' He reached out to grab the man but before he could do so he had vanished back into the throng and was gone.

For a moment O'Sullivan sat there, slumped in thought, then he said, as the jeep started to move again, 'Did you see that, sir?'

'What?' Stirling asked.

'A Gippo asked me for a light, but I'm sure he wasn't one bit interested in that. What he wanted to see was my cap badge. That's what interested him.'

Stirling bit his bottom lip. 'You might well be right. Cairo is full of German agents and sympathizers and by now the Hun will know we're the only parachute unit in the Middle East. Yes, Bill, it looks as if they are on to us already.' He shrugged. 'Nothing much we can do about it, I suppose. All right Dawson, carry on.'

Ten minutes later they arrived at GHQ. It was clear as they waited in the great high-ceilinged waiting-room of the headquarters, that it, too, was not free from fear and tension. Dispatch-riders, covered in desert dust, kept coming and going hurriedly. Young staff officers with worried faces and thick files under their arms hurried back and forth. Telephones jingled incessantly. And from the open door of the office opposite, an irate voice was saying, 'You've got to get that battalion up there at once. If you don't, God knows what will happen to the line. We're just holding on by our bloody teeth at the moment.'

'Typical staff wallahs,' Mayne snorted scornfully, 'Fill their pants as soon as they hear a shot fired in anger.'

'Shut up, Paddy,' Stirling hissed urgently. 'They'll sling us out on our ear in half a mo.'

'The gentlemen from the—er—Special Air Service?' a cultivated voice queried.

They looked round as one.

A cheerful young officer in an immaculate gabardine uniform, was looking down at them.

Mayne's face set in a sneer. He didn't say anything, but O'Sullivan knew what he was thinking—typical staff wallah, enjoying himself in this Cairo fuckhole.

'The General will see you now. He can just make it for five minutes. Then you are to proceed to Room 101 where Colonel Keyes of the 11th Commando is waiting for you for a further briefing.'

Hurriedly the three of them rose to their

102

feet and followed the elegant young officer down the corridors to a door, where a sentry was standing, bayonet fixed to his rifle, as if he half expected to be fighting to defend the General's life at any moment. The staff officer knocked. A deep voice said, 'Come' and they went in.

A very tall officer sat behind the desk, handsome in a very English kind of a way, with deep lines of worry etched in his long face. They saluted and he said, 'Stand at ease.' He gave them a little smile and added, ' 'Fraid I've not much time. Bit of a crisis on my hands at the moment. But I *did* want to have a look at the cut of your jib.' His faint smile vanished. 'I must frankly confess that I don't like this op, Stirling,' he addressed himself to the head of the SAS. 'It's not—er—well cricket, but it's been ordered by Mr Churchill himself. He said it's the only way to stop the rot in the Middle East and what the PM says goes, I'm afraid.'

'What is the operation, sir?' Paddy Mayne asked unabashed.

The Auk looked at him sharply, as if he might rebuke him, but he didn't. Instead he said, 'Well, I suppose you're going to find out soon enough. You and the LRDG people are going to provide the support for selected men from Colonel Keyes' 11th Commando.' He paused, as if he were reluctant to utter the words aloud. 'And it's going to be the job of Colonel Keyes' group to capture General Rommel.'

O'Sullivan gasped and Mayne shot him a significant look.

'And if they can't capture Rommel,' the Auk gave a little shrug, 'then they'll have to deal with him in another way. The PM's given his permission.'

'You mean kill him?' Mayne blurted out brutally.

Auchinleck looked suddenly unhappy. 'Yes,' he stuttered, 'I suppose that is what is meant. It's a bad business, but obviously the PM thinks that with Rommel—er—dealt with, the heart will go out of the *Afrikakorps*.'

O'Sullivan felt sorry for the big army commander. He was obviously a very decent man of the old school, who hated the idea of what amounted to assassination.

But if Auchinleck hated the idea, Stirling didn't. He said, 'I think that's the way to do it, sir, if I may be so bold. Getting rid of Rommel won't only deal the *Afrikakorps* a blow will also hearten our chaps. There's been too much made of this "Desert Fox" sort of thing. After all the chap has become a legend among our troops. It's time we cut the Germans down to size.'

'I suppose you're right, Stirling,' the Auk said, but O'Sullivan was sure he wasn't convinced. 'All right then, I won't detain you any longer. You'll be wanting to speak to Colonel Keyes.'

As they rose and saluted, O'Sullivan flashed a swift look at Mayne and it was obvious from the scowl on his craggy face meeting Keyes was the last thing he wanted to do.

Colonel Keyes and some of his officers of the 11th Commando were waiting for them when they arrived at Room 101. He was a tall, very thin man, his face hollowed out to a bronzed death's head, a small moustache adorning his upper lip as if it had been drawn on by pencil. Stirling saluted and introduced his two companions. 'Lieutenants O'Sullivan and Mayne, sir.'

Keyes shook O'Sullivan's hand, but refused to take that of Mayne. 'We've met before,' he said coldly. 'Now then,' he said briskly, 'let's get down to business.' He turned and pointed to the big map of Mediterranean coastline pinned up on the easel behind him. 'Our plan, as you've already heard from the C-in-C is to kidnap or kill General Rommel.'

O'Sullivan told himself the commando colonel certainly didn't mince words. He came straight to the point.

THE ROMMEL ATTACK - THE PLAN

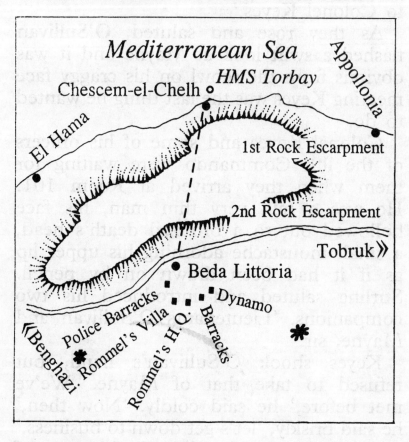

Mediterranean Sea

HMS Torbay

Chescem-el-Chelh

Appollonia

El Hama

1st Rock Escarpment

2nd Rock Escarpment

Tobruk ≫

Beda Littoria

Dynamo

《Benghazi

Police Barracks

Rommel's Villa

Rommel's H.Q.

Barracks

- - - Keys' Approach from *HMS Torbay*

✳ SAS Position

✳ LRDG Rendezvous

'Four detachments of commandos will be landed by sub—here at Cheschem-el-Chelb. One group under my command will head for the house thought occupied by Rommel at Sidi Rafa as the Egyptians call it, or Beda Littorio as the Eyeties rc-named it. The other three groups will sabotage the Eyetie telephone and communications system throughout the whole area. The object is to seal off the area from Beda Littoria until we're clear of the place.'

He let the information sink in before continuing. 'Now the Navy can't risk the subs which will take us in, by trying to take us off again, once the balloon goes up. The place will obviously be swarming with Hun planes and ships. So we shall have to escape overland.' He looked hard at Stirling and Steele who had just entered. 'Here then is where the LRDG and what do you call yourselves?' he looked at Stirling.

Stirling frowned. He knew Keyes knew the name of his command. It was a deliberate provocation. 'The Special Air Service,' Stirling growled and O'Sullivan could literally feel Paddy Mayne's rising anger. He prayed that the big Irishman wouldn't lose his temper. That would mean disaster.

'Oh yes, well we'll have to footslog into the desert to a RV—say—about ten miles from Rommel's HQ where you, Major Steele, will be waiting. I shall leave it to you to select what you think is the best place for a rendezvous.'

Steele nodded his understanding.

Keyes turned to Stirling. 'Your chaps will provide the fire power to cover us, Stirling, between Beda Littoria and wherever the RV is to be. We will be only lightly armed and I suspect we shall have used up most of our ammo by the time we're finished with Rommel and the Eyetie communication system. We'll have to depend upon you from there onwards. Is that clear?'

'Very, sir,' Stirling said coldly and O'Sullivan realized that tension was already building up between the two officers, both of whom were empire builders in their way, after all, Keyes was only twenty-four and he was a light colonel already. The fact that Mayne was a member of Stirling's new unit didn't help much either, he told himself.

'Good. Now then gentlemen, I won't waste any further words. We shall split up into groups now and get on with our individual planning. But let me emphasize this before we do so.' He looked hard at Mayne. 'Everything will now depend upon teamwork. Everything will have to work precisely if we are to succeed. There can be no place for prima donnas in this operation.'

Mayne went red with suppressed fury. But now O'Sullivan was no longer watching the big Irishman. His gaze was fixed on Colonel Keyes, for he had just noticed something that he had not seen before in the latter's face. Kcyes had the mark of death on him.

Chapter Two

'I'm going out on the razzle,' Mayne growled, as they left the GHQ. The planning of the operation had taken most of the day and now it was almost evening. Over the Nile the sun was beginning to set and everywhere the lights were going on. Already the streets were filling with the evening traffic and the harsh guttural cries of the hawkers and beggars. 'I want to wash the damned taste of that bugger Keyes out of my mouth.'

O'Sullivan frowned. He knew what Paddy meant. Throughout the long planning session there had been tension in the air all the time. Keyes had been very full of himself and neither Stirling nor Mayne had taken kindly to that. Twice Major Steele had been forced to intervene and calm the situation down.

109

'What about you, Bill?' Paddy asked. 'Do you fancy getting stinking?'

O'Sullivan shook his head. 'No thanks, Paddy. I'll just have a drink at Shepheard's. Remember we're off back to the oasis at the crack of dawn.'

Mayne shrugged. 'Have it your own way, Bill. But I'm going to get a skinful. See you later.' With that he was gone pushing his way through the crowds of officers, leaving the GHQ, without any regard to their rank.

O'Sullivan grinned a little and told himself that Paddy Mayne was a card. He didn't give a damn about anything or anybody.

The big bar at Shepheard's was packed. O'Sullivan had forced his way through the crowds of drunken Australian soldiers peering in at the doorway, the squint-eyed pimps, crying 'Cap'n, Cap'n, you want my sister. All pink inside like white lady' and beggars holding up their skinny black arms for coins, to find the place crowded with staff officers in elegant uniforms, men from the desert in scruffy shorts and shirts and leave-men, dressed in skin-tight cavalry overalls. He fought his way to the long bar and ordered a mint julep.

When he had first drunk at Shepheard's, he had found it strange that everyone drunk mint juleps which he thought was very American, but an older officer had enlightened him, 'It was Nelson's favourite drink. It's been going on since the time he won the Battle of Nile out here.' O'Sullivan had wondered whether the story was true or not. At all events, however, everyone at Shepheard's always drank mint juleps.

He took his drink and sipping it carefully, enjoying its coldness after the heat of the day, he got out of the way of the throng at the bar and looked for somewhere to sit.

'Over here, Lieutenant,' a slightly accented woman's voice called nearby.

He turned. A really beautiful woman was smiling at him encouragingly and patting the empty seat next to her with her elegant hand.

'Me?' he asked a little startled.

The woman was perhaps thirty, but she was certainly something to look at: a carefully made up face under dark hair, with a splendid figure under an expensive silk gown. She was smoking a Turkish cigarette, sweet smelling and highly perfumed, through a long ivory cigarette holder. Again she patted the empty seat and smiled at him with dark eyes full of promise.

O'Sullivan gulped a little. Was she one of those high-class whores who worked bars like that at Shepheard's, or the wife of some high-ranking officer who was looking for a bit of fun? He didn't know. But it wasn't every day that a lowly second-lieutenant got a chance like this. So he went across. He gave her a short nervous bow, feeling a bit of a fool as he did so, and introduced himself, 'Lieutenant Bill O'Sullivan. But you can call me Bill, if you like.'

'Bill, you shall be,' she said in that delightfully accented English of hers and pressed his hand encouragingly with hers. 'And you can call me Yvonne.' As she leaned closer to him he caught a whiff of expensive perfume and he told himself that she couldn't be a whore. Pros didn't make the kind of money needed to buy perfume like that. But who was she?

It was almost as if she could read his mind for she said with a laugh, 'I am married. But my husband is away in the desert. In fact, he has been away a long time, *too* long,' she looked at him significantly and he told himself he had been well and truly picked up. He felt his pulse quicken and a sudden thickening of his loins. He looked down at her glass, which was almost empty. 'Could I get you another drink?' he asked.

'No thank you,' she said, 'It's far too noisy here. But when you have finished your drink, I shall get *you* a drink. In my

112

apartment. I think it will be much more pleasant there, not so many rough, loud men. What do you say?'

O'Sullivan's hand shook a little with excitement as he raised his glass and took a quick gulp. 'I'd say that would be very kind of you,' he said, hardly recognizing his own voice.

'It is not difficult to be *kind*,' she emphasized the word with a fluttering of her long eyelashes, 'to such brave boys as you. After all the hardships you undergo in the desert, you deserve to be spoiled.'

'Well, thank you,' he stuttered foolishly, downing his drink in short quick sips, while she looked at him encouragingly, as if she just couldn't wait to be 'kind' to him...

Her apartment was in a fashionable block in Sharia Nabatat on Zamalek Island. The furniture wasn't the usual bamboo stuff made in Egypt, but elegant imported European pieces and there were servants, too. But once the maid had taken her wrap and the white-robed houseman Achmed, in claret-coloured tarbush, pantaloons and a splendid salta with wide slashed sleeves, had brought in the bottle of champagne in the silver ice bucket, they were dismissed.

She said, 'Now relax. Look around if you want. There is a splendid view of Cairo from the balcony. Open the champagne now, if you wish. I shan't be more than a minute.' With that she was gone into a room he suspected was her bedroom.

Idly he wandered around the place. For a few moments he stared out across the Nile, the red, green and white lights of the buildings and cars reflected in the viscous surface of the great river. For there was no blackout in Cairo. The Germans didn't want to offend the Eygptians, many of whom, especially the educated classes, supported the Germans and regarded them as 'liberators'.

He moved back inside again and walked around, staring at the many photographs adorning the walls. They were mostly of Yvonne: lounging in a skin-tight white bathing suit at the pool at the Gezira Sporting Club, having dinner at Shepheard's in an elegant evening gown, at the racetrack on Zamalek Island, posed in a large floppy hat, floral dressed and peering through binoculars. Obviously Yvonne belonged to Cairo's wealthiest class.

But who was her damned husband? O'Sullivan asked himself, a little frustrated, as he continued his viewing, no noise coming from outside now save for the soft lap-lap of the water.

He stopped suddenly. There was a picture of Yvonne looking radiant in beach pyjamas, a glass in her hand, beaming at the camera on some summer beach or other. But this time it wasn't Yvonne's brilliant white-toothed smile or large breasts jutting through the thin silk of the pyjamas which caught his attention. It was the huge man standing protectively near her, his brawny arm wrapped round her waist. The man was virtually black, his face scarred like those he had seen of Sudanese soldiers.

She caught him unawares as she opened the door noiselessly and saw him gazing at the photograph. 'My husband,' she said simply, 'the General.'

He turned round and gasped. She was clad in a low cut silk negligee which revealed every curve of her beautiful body to perfection.

She caught the look in his eyes and smiled softly, 'You like it?' she asked softly.

'Oh gosh, yes!'

'And what's inside it as well?' she added a little slyly.

'Yes...of course,' he choked, feeling very excited and flushed.

'Then come and kiss me, show me that you really do appreciate me.'

He was unable to control himself any longer. He grabbed her and pressed her roughly to him, feeling those splendid breasts nuzzling against his chest, his

115

breath coming in short gasps. Greedily he pressed his lips against hers. Her tongue slid inside his mouth and he shivered with delight. She then released herself from his arms, pushing him away gently. 'You are a naughty boy, aren't you?' she teased. 'Now be a darling and open the bubbly. We've got all night, haven't we?'

O'Sullivan's sexual experience had been limited. A tart in Liverpool just before his regiment had embarked. He had told himself he had to lose his virginity before he went overseas. A three day leave in Cairo spent with an ugly VAD nurse who had not allowed him to see her undress and had warned him severely before they had gone to bed together, 'Now, I don't want anything dirty. I know you dreadful men and your nasty tricks. Just straightforward love-making, do you hear?'

And an Arab whore in Alexandria when he had gone up there to pick up some new trucks for the regiment from the docks. For days afterwards he had worried whether or not he had picked up VD from her.

Now, however, for the first time he was experiencing real love-making of the kind of sexual intensity he had hardly dreamed existed. At times she was lascivious and obscene. She thrust her soft naked body close to his, offering her nipples to be kissed temptingly, whispering huskily, 'You

116

want to fuck me, don't you. But you shall kiss these first, suckle, fondle them for a long time.' Other times she was driven into a mad frenzy, face distorted in the soft red light and lathered in sweat, as she moaned and cried, her red nails tearing into his buttocks as he thrust himself into her over and over again.

Once he awoke from an exhausted doze to find her sobbing softly. But her sadness didn't last long. Soon her pink tongue was licking the inside of his ear while her cunning little hand was working on his flaccid organ, as she whispered knowingly, 'I know you want it again...you can't get enough of it, can you?'

And he couldn't.

She woke him from an exhausted sleep at five that morning. The sun had just slipped over the horizon to the east and was beginning to colour the dawn sky a blood red. She was already bathed and made-up and next to the bed she had placed a silver tray with a pot of Turkish coffee and a plate of fresh croissants.

She kissed him lightly on the lips and said as he yawned and ran his hands through his tousled hair, 'Good morning, Bill, my chauffeur will take you to GHQ. The car is already outside. First have something to drink and eat. You're going to miss breakfast, I'm afraid.' She lowered

117

her eyes and simpered, 'I hope I'm worth it?'

'Of course, you are,' he said gallantly and reached out for her. She avoided his grasp, her breasts shimmering delightfully under the sheer white silk of her gown.

'Enough of that,' she said, 'You've got to go off now and fight the big war. No time for love-making. She dropped her mocking tone for a moment. 'But you will be careful, Bill won't you? I don't want you to get hurt.' For some reason which O'Sullivan couldn't fathom, she looked just then at the portrait of herself and her husband.

Minutes later she was kissing him goodbye in the dawn coolness, saying, 'I hope you won't have to parachute this time. They tell me it's dreadfully dangerous.'

'Shall I see you again?' he asked urgently, not really hearing her remark.

'Of course, of course,' she said. 'Now you must go. Achmed.'

'*Iewa, Ta'ala* plees, madam.' Smoothly the driver drew the big Packard away from the curb and set off for the bridge.

O'Sullivan flung a glance through the little rear window but she had already gone inside again. Perhaps it was too cool for her, clad as she was in the thin robe.

It was only when they were nearing

GHQ that her remark about parachuting came to mind. What had she said: 'I hope you won't have to parachute this time.' He frowned puzzled. Why had she said 'this time.' Then they were passing the sentries who had clicked to attention and he was returning their salute, the remark forgotten almost instantly.

Chapter Three

'Up came a spider, sat down beside her, whipped his old bazooka, and this is what he said,' Dawson was singing monotonously as he drove the jeep, bumping and jolting over the potholed desert road, 'big balls, small balls, balls as big as yer head, give 'em a twist and swing 'em right over yer head...'

Next to him the three officers sat slumped in the morning heat, each one wrapped in a cocoon of his own thoughts. O'Sullivan was reliving the excitement of that night together with Yvonne, mind in a turmoil as he did so, telling himself he had never had an experience like that before. Once in the middle of the night when he had felt he could not make love any more, she had taken his flaccid organ into her mouth gently and when it was hardening she had slipped it between the moist lips of her vagina. She had worked it up and down between them till it was really hard and when he had wanted to thrust it into her, she had not let him. She had continued to rub it up and down between her legs until he thought he couldn't stand it any more. It was then that she had allowed him to enter her and he had exploded in a great body-shuddering climax.

O'Sullivan shook his head and forced himself not to think of her. He felt if he did, he would become excited once more and that would be embarrassing. He turned to Paddy Mayne who was sitting next to him, his craggy face black and gloomy. 'Penny for them, Paddy?' he asked.

'What?' the Irishman grunted and then added, 'Not much. I was just thinking I don't like this Rommel stunt and I don't like the way that Keyes is going to do it. He'll get the limelight and we won't get a look-in. We're just a bloody flank guard.' He spat over the side of the open jeep angrily.

Stirling, who sat next to Dawson, who was launching into the second verse of his dirty dirge with 'I've got a luvverly bunch o' coconuts. I've got a luvverly bunch o' balls', snapped, 'Oh put a sock in it, Dawson. Please.'

Up ahead of them Smith 175 who was driving the new jeep, they were taking back to the Oasis, was slowing down. There was some sort of barricade across the road, being manned by armed Egyptian police and soldiers.

Stirling said, 'Paddy, I think you're wrong. I agree with you that Keyes is wanting to make himself the hero of this thing, but if he pulls it off, we'll get some of the kudos and after our first fiasco we badly need success—' He broke off and stared to his front again. 'Hello, what's going on? The Gippos have ordered Smith 175 out of the jeep.'

'The cheeky Gippo sods,' Dawson snorted. 'They can't do that to my mucker. Not the Gippos.'

O'Sullivan shot a glance to his front over Dawson's shoulder. The first jeep had come to a halt and a burly Egyptian policeman, with the three stripes of a sergeant on his arm, was ordering Smith 175 out, levelling his rifle at him threateningly. Automatically O'Sullivan loosened the flap of his pistol holster and made sure that his .38 was cocked. There was something fishy going on here, he told himself grimly. Normally the Egyptian police and army stayed clear of British soldiers. They were more than likely to get a kick in the pants if they tackled British soldiers, especially those who had come back from 'up the blue'.

Stirling evidently thought the same, for he said, 'I don't like this one bit, chaps. I don't think they'd try this one on, if they didn't outnumber us four to one. Dawson stop here, let's see what their little game is.'

Dawson braked, face red with suppressed anger. Next to him, Stirling craned his head forward as two of the Egyptians started to search Smith, patting his body up and down, while the sergeant covered them with his rifle. Others were waving for the stationary jeep to come on. Obviously they were going to be subjected to the same treatment.

'What bloody cheek!' Paddy Mayne fumed, clenching his fists angrily. 'What bloody right have they got to stop us. Christ, they couldn't fight their way out of a wet paper bag.'

'Dawson go on, *slowly*. Bill over the side now. We'll pretend to kowtow to them tamely. When we halt, up you come with yer pistol. If they give us any of the old acid, blow a hole in the sods.'

'Sir.' O'Sullivan knew the drill. Covered from the view of the Egyptians by the bulk of Guardsman Dawson and Stirling, he dropped over the side and clutching the spare wheel, drew his revolver.

Dawson started to move forward again at a snail's pace. Tensely O'Sullivan waited till he would spring into action. Up ahead, the sergeant, satisfied that Smith 175 wasn't armed, was pointing at the blue and white parachute wings sewn on to the shoulder of Smith's khaki shirt and chattering away rapidly in Arabic.

'You know,' Stirling hissed. 'It looks to me as if they're pinpointing us because we're parachutists...perhaps because we're the SAS.' He sucked his top teeth thoughtfully. 'It's almost as if they knew we were coming down this road this morning.' Not taking his eyes off the Egyptians to his front, he called. 'We're nearly there, Bill. Get on your mark. You know the drill.'

O'Sullivan clenched his jaw and prepared himself for what was to come. The jeep rolled slowly to a halt. The big sergeant grinned showing a mouthful of bright white teeth. 'All the Stirling Misters' he said. 'We bin waiting you.'

At the back of the jeep, O'Sullivan heard the words quite clearly. Instinctively he knew they had walked into a trap. There was no time for questions—words—now. Action was all that counted. Even before Stirling started to get out of the jeep, he dropped to the sand and crouching there, covered by the back of the little vehicle, he fired.

On the edge of the crowd of Egyptians, a little man in khaki groaned suddenly and clapped his hand to his shoulder, from which blood had started to arc in a scarlet jet. O'Sullivan fired again and another of the ambushers dropped to the sand.

In that same instant Stirling and Mayne pulled out their pistols. 'Right drop your weapons,' Stirling yelled harshly to the surprised and frightened Egyptians. 'Come on now—hurry it up!'

The ambushers did as they were ordered swiftly, all except the sergeant. He seemed reluctant to lower his rifle which was still levelled at Smith 175's chest. Paddy Mayne acted. He sprang out of the jeep. With one big hand, he grabbed the muzzle of the sergeant's rifle. With the other, he smashed a blow into the Egyptian's face which would have felled him if Paddy had not been holding on to his rifle. The sergeant's nose broke with an audible crack. Blood started to stream from his shattered nostrils. 'Now then will ye drop the bloody bondhook?' Mayne cried, eyes blazing.

The Egyptian let the rifle fall to the sand. He staggered back, moaning softly, hands held to his shattered nose, blood seeping through his fingers.

Dawson got out of the jeep and stared at the bunch of crestfallen Egyptians. 'Nice turn up for the books, sir,' he said to Stirling. 'What do you make of it? Why should the Gippos have tried to stop us?'

Stirling looked hard at the battered sergeant, 'You speak English,' he thundered. 'Who ordered you to stop us? And why?'

'*Effendi*,' the man wailed thickly, 'I do as I told. The *Bimbashi* ordered me to stop you here.'

'Shut up you fool,' a thin educated voice snapped.

Stirling shot a look at the crowd of subdued frightened Egyptians and spotted the speaker at once. He, too, was a policeman, but he wasn't cowed like the rest. He had dropped his weapon, but his face was hard and his dark eyes blazed with rage as he stared at Stirling. 'You come here,' Stirling ordered.

For a moment, it appeared the man might refuse to move. Dawson didn't hesitate. He gave the policeman a kick who went stumbling forward to fall on his knees at Stirling's feet.

'Who are you?' Stirling demanded while O'Sullivan stared at the policeman. He was beefier than the rest and O'Sullivan could

125

see the powerful muscular arms of a man who was used to exercise and plenty of good food. This man, he told himself, was not one of the usual downtrodden skinny Delta Egyptians, who made up most of their forces. He was cut above them.

'Nouri—Lieutenant Nouri,' the defiant policeman said reluctantly.

'Well, what's all this about? What's your little game?' Stirling snapped, as he towered above the Egyptian.

'I am a patriot,' he shot back, no fear, only anger in his face. 'One who is fighting to free Egypt from you British. You British turn your machine guns on a crowd of unarmed natives, put up your Union Jack and say "this is ours". Afterwards you build a few roads, a school or two and send rich men's sons to Oxford so that they become your lackeys. Then you begin to loot your new conquest. You give yourself a mission which is a cover for twenty-five per cent dividends annually and safe controlled markets.' His mouth twisted in bitter scorn. 'It's nothing to do with King and Country and your damned white man's burden. It's just got to do with money—'

Paddy Mayne reached back his hamlike fist and hit the man so hard that he staggered and almost fell to the ground. 'No more bloody lectures from you, Gippo,' he roared. 'Answer the bloody question, man. What's your bloody game?'

'All right, Paddy,' Stirling restrained the Irishman, as the Egyptian officer wiped the blood from his split lip. 'We'll question him further at the oasis. Smith 175 and Dawson.'

'Sir?'

'Take the bolts from these chaps' rifles and put them in the jeep. Then we're off again. I don't think it's wise to hang around here for too long.' He gave the empty desert road behind them a quick glance, as if he half expected more Egyptians to come barrelling down it. 'You, Bill, take care of the prisoner. Use his own belt and tie his hands behind his back.'

'Yes, sir.'

Hurriedly while the two guardsmen took the bolts from the morose Egyptians' rifles and tossed them into the back of Smith's jeep, O'Sullivan tied the prisoner's hands tightly behind his back, conscious all the while of the naked hate which emanated from the Egyptian. He was conscious, too, that there was some connection between the planned ambush and Yvonne back in Cairo. What, he didn't know. But it was there—definitely.

127

Chapter Four

'Bagnold's our Arabic expert. He speaks the lingo like a native,' Steele of the LRDG said. 'He's at work on Nouri now.'

They squatted in the shade cast by one of the palm trees, listening to the gentle rippling of the oasis' pool. It was still very hot though evening was approaching, and the SAS officers were glad of the shade of the trees.

'Nouri's a tight-lipped bugger,' Steele said. 'But if anyone can get anything it will be Bagnold. He's reputed to get even a mummy to talk.'

Nobody laughed. They were all too concerned by the problem posed by the Egyptian police lieutenant. For it was obvious, even at this stage, a junior officer of the Egyptian Police wouldn't have dared to have stopped them unless he had received orders from someone high up to do so.

'Has Bagnold got anything at all out of him so far?'

Before Steele had chance to answer, Paddy Mayne snorted, 'If you'd leave him with me for half an hour I'd have that Gippo singing like a bloody canary.'

O'Sullivan grinned and told himself that it was fortunate for the Egyptian that they hadn't let Paddy loose on him.

'Bagnold says that he's got out of him that they were definitely looking for you SAS chaps. They had been told to look out for British soldiers wearing parachute wings. And your lot, Stirling, is the only one in the whole of the Middle East to wear those wings.'

Again O'Sullivan remembered Yvonne's parting words. He decided he couldn't remain silent on the matter any longer, though he still couldn't see the connection. 'Sir,' he said a little uneasily, feeling himself going red already, 'I think I might have something there—about those parachute wings.'

They turned and stared at him curiously. Behind them a camel started to bray raucously and O'Sullivan had to raise his voice above the racket the beast was making. 'The night we were in Cairo, sir,' he said slowly, 'I was picked up by an Egyptian woman in the bar at Shepheards' Hotel.'

'Lucky dog,' Stirling said enviously. 'Young chaps have all the luck, even when they don't really know what it's all about.'

'Be quiet, Stirling,' Steele said sharply. 'Go on, O'Sullivan.'

Swiftly O'Sullivan told what had happened, glad to able to get it off his chest at last.

They listened attentively as he told his story and how Yvonne's husband was supposed to be at 8th Army HQ's and how she had hoped that he wouldn't have to use a parachute. He ended with a lame, 'Well, thought I ought to mention it because I think I led these chaps to us.'

There was silence when he had finished his account, broken only by the sound of an Arab whacking the camel with his stick. Perhaps the beast had drunk too much water. The Arabs rationed their beasts strictly.

Finally, Steele, who had been out in Egypt right from the start of the war and who was the most experienced of them all, broke the brooding silence with, 'This general fellow, the husband—supposedly —of your Yvonne woman, might well be one of those groups of Egyptian Army officers who want us out of their country. Only last month that playboy king of theirs—Farouk—told our ambassador chap, he wished the British would pick their white man's burden up and go away. Well, everybody knows that fat playboy with pornographic movies and little girls won't ever do anything about it. But the Army might. Already they've attempted to make contact with the Germans and they are actively spying against us.'

He paused to let his words sink in and O'Sullivan said, 'But why would they be interested in our op sir? What's it got to do with the Gippos?'

Steele said, 'I think it's because Rommel is seen as some kind of hero...a German who has taken on the British and rubbed their noses in the you know what. Even the poor Delta Gippos know who Rommel is. Now,' he frowned, as if he were having difficulty formulating his words, 'if we bump off Rommel, that figurehead goes, and those Gippo plotters might loose the support of the rank-and-file. That's my guess anyway. So if they've rumbled us in Cairo, they might as well do their best to stop us before it's too late.'

'*Sir*,' the voice cried urgently twenty yards away. 'Sir... Major Steele, sir!'

Steele swung round hastily. 'What is it?' he called to the air sentry who crouched behind the bren gun, mounted on a tripod.

'Aircraft three o'clock, sir,' the sentry yelled back.

Steele shaded his eyes against the glare of the sinking sun and stared at the aeroplane, outlined a stark black against the red glow of the sun. 'Christ Almighty, no mistaking the silhouette of that one.

O'Sullivan followed the direction of his gaze. 'Hell's bells!' he exclaimed, as he recognized the machine as well. *'Fieseler Storch.'* He had seen the monoplane with its radial engine often enough when he had been with the Grenadiers. The Germans used them as spotters. They were immensely flexible. They could fly at ground level at not much faster than the speed of the average civilian car. They saw everything.

Steele obviously knew that, for he cupped his hands around his mouth and cried. 'Everyone hit the deck! Faces down! Into the shade!'

The men reacted as they had been trained—at once. They flung themselves downwards in the sand under cover of the palms, while Arabs staying at the oasis stared at them in amazement, wondering why they were doing so.

The German reconnaissance plane came nearer and nearer. Glancing up O'Sullivan could just see the black outline of the pilot in his canopy which sparkled in the rays of the setting sun. An instant later the *Fieseler Storch* was directly above the oasis, the pilot flying just above stalling speed.

Now he started to circle the area, while the Arabs stared upwards and pointed or waved in some cases, babbling away in their guttural Arabic, for they had rarely seen a plane this far south.

'The sod's on to us,' Paddy Mayne hissed, as if he were afraid he might be overhead by the German pilot searching for them. 'I'm sure he is.'

'I don't know,' Steele said uncertainly. 'It's a long time since we had a Jerry plane over here. Duck, here he comes again.'

This time the enemy pilot was coming in dangerously low, his prop wash making the palm fronds whip back and forth, showering those hiding below with dates.

'The trucks are well camouflaged,' Steele hissed. 'But he might well see. Then the fat'll be really in the fire.'

Next moment the plane roared over them, dragging its black shadow like that of some monstrous bird behind it. The roar of its engine grew. The pilot was speeding the plane up and this time he didn't come to have another look. They waited there, faces still to the ground, making no movement. They could well have been dead. Finally the air sentry said, 'I think he's done a bunk for good, sir.'

They roused themselves and stared to

the north. The *Fieseler Storch* was a mere black dot against the red wash of the evening sky. In a few moments it would vanish altogether.

'What do you think?' Stirling asked Steele. 'Did he spot us? He seems to be in a damn fine hurry to get back to his own lines.'

Steele pursed his lips thoughtfully and didn't answer for a moment. Then he said, 'Stirling, rouse your men and I'll do the same with my chaps. There's a wadi six miles from here where we'll be safe. I'm not sure but I have an idea that the Huns'll be back before this night is over. And it's better to be away from the oasis if they are.'

Ten minutes later, all their gear piled hastily into the trucks and jeeps, they were on their way to the wadi, leaving the surprised Arab nomads in the sole possession of the oasis.

It was two hours later when they were having the final brew up of the day, dixies filled with rich strong brown tea and others with 'M and V', meat and vegetable stew, plus lots of tinned potatoes, when they heard the distant roar coming from the north. 'Dowse the fires,' officers ordered urgently. 'And dish out the char and grub straightaway.'

Hurriedly sand was poured into the

134

tins which contained the sand and petrol mix with which they cooked their meals. Mess tins and mugs were produced hastily and while they ate and drank, the men crouched in the shelter of the rocky wadi and waited tensely for what would soon happen. For all of them, even the dullest, realized they had been spotted at the oasis and the Germans were coming back—in force!

'There they are,' Paddy Mayne shouted suddenly. 'Over there.'

They swung round. The approaching planes were clearly outlined a stark black against the night sky. There were nine of them, a whole squadron, and Mayne identified them almost immediately, *'Junkers,'* he yelled, as they thundered ever closer, *'Junkers 88.'*

O'Sullivan nodded his agreement. He, too, recognized the slim, two engined, long-range German bombers. And they were heading straight for the oasis.

A moment later the squadron leader started dropping flares. They burst in mid-air, turning night into day, as they floated down slowly, casting an ice-white, incandescent hue over the ground below.

The second wave came in now. In that eerie glowing light, the watchers could see the bomb-doors open. Moments later there was the spine-chilling whine of bombs

135

hurtling to the ground.

'Cor ferk a duck,' Dawson gasped, 'I even feel sorry for them frigging towelheads over there.'

The ground trembled as the first of the bombs struck home. Suddenly the oasis erupted. Great scarlet stabs of flame stabbed the night. Palms flew into the air. Dark smoke shot upwards in a great column.

Still yet another wave of three came rumbling in to drop their deadly load and Stirling said grimly, 'They are certainly out to make mincemeat of anything living below. Look at that!' In another flash of vivid red they saw a headless camel whirling round and around as it flew upwards before disappearing as the scarlet glare vanished.

Later they realized that the deadly raid must have gone on for only a matter of minutes, but at this moment it seemed to continue for ever. And then the Germans were moving off, leaving huge fires burning below and in the desert stillness, as they vanished they could hear the faint cries and wails of those who had survived that devasting air raid.

'Thank God, we moved when we did,' Steele was saying in an awed voice, 'Our goose would have certainly been cooked,' when another voice cut in urgently.

'Sir,' it was Bagnold. 'Nouri has started to sing. He has just seen what happened to his people at the oasis. He has just told me he never thought the Germans would do anything as terrible as that. He's ready to tell us anything we want to know, sir.'

'Excellent, excellent,' Steele said happily, forgetting the tragedy of the oasis, 'Wheel him up, Bagnold, smartish and let's hear what all this business is about.'

'Yvonne was a whore,' Nouri said bitterly, five minutes later. He had been weeping earlier and his face was still tear-stained but bitter. 'The general was a lot older. He found her in a *maison particulier* in Alexandria. He liked her and bought her.'

The others looked amused and interested. O'Sullivan blushed. 'Fancy,' Stirling said, '*bought* her. That's rare.'

'He spoiled her and in the end she began to help the cause.'

'The cause?' Steele echoed.

'The cause of Egypt,' Nouri said with sudden pride, 'which I still believe in. But our cause will not be helped by those murderous Germans. They are worse than the English. They look down upon us Egyptians, too.'

'All right, all right,' Paddy Mayne said, 'keep your shirt on. Get on with it. What's

137

this general of yours, who buys women from knocking shops, got to do with the Jerries?'

'The general is the Egyptian Army's liaison officer at your 8th Army GHQ. He might be an old roue, but he is a patriot and has sharp eyes and ears which he keeps open.'

'So you mean he spies on our plans, eh?' Steele said grimly. 'A traitor!'

'Exactly, Major,' Nouri replied. 'But he is not a traitor to us. As I have already said, he works for our cause.'

'Go on then,' Steele urged.

'Soon it is hoped that we shall be able to send him to General Rommel personally where he will reveal the dispositions of your 8th Army to him for the Germans next offensive.' He coughed and spat bitterly into the sand. 'Though now I am not so sure about it. When Rommel comes to Cairo, will he come as a liberator or a new tyrant, another one carrying the white man's burden? We thought that you men of the SAS knew something of what was going on and we were determined to stop—'

He halted abruptly. In the distance there again came the roar of heavy motors.

'Christ Almighty,' Paddy Mayne moaned, 'can't the sods get enough? *They're coming back!*'

Chapter Five

'There they are!' someone shouted and pointed to the sky.

Hastily O'Sullivan started to count the number of dark shapes approaching the bombed-out oasis, at a much slower rate than the *Junkers* for some reason he couldn't fathom. 'There are nine of them again,' he said.

'Overdoing it a bit,' Paddy Mayne said a little puzzled. 'Another whole squadron. The Jerries must think we're very bloody important to send another squadron to do us in. You would have thought the first lot had given the oasis enough of a pasting.'

'How thorough the Germans are,' Nouri said bitterly, watching with the rest of them as the enemy planes came closer. 'They want to make sure that none of my people survive.' Again he spat angrily into the sand at his feet.

'Something strange though,' Stirling said suddenly.

'What?' Steele asked.

'I can see the exhaust flames from the first three planes, but not from the other six. I can't figure it out,' Stirling answered. 'Very strange.'

'Look,' Smith 175 standing nearby yelled, 'that first plane's having some trouble.'

They followed the direction of his outstretched hand. Smith was right. The lead plane's engine was beginning to cough and splutter. Angry red sparks flew from its port engine.

'Serves the sod right,' Smith 175 yelled in delight. 'Couldn't happen to a nicer bloke.' The plane shook violently and he chortled, 'That's the stuff to give the troops.'

Abruptly the lead plane began to go into a shallow dive. Something they couldn't identify swished through the air with a sound like a great whip being cracked. The two planes behind the one in trouble rose sharply and the first plane came out of its dive a little. Then still coughing and spluttering, it disappeared behind the hill beyond the wadi.

Now the two following planes began to circle, silently ominous, like two great sinister hawks, and finally the watchers tumbled to the nature of those strangely silent aircraft. 'Gliders,' Paddy bellowed in alarm, 'they're ruddy troop-carrying gliders. They're about to attack the oasis with troops!'

Steele didn't hesitate. He cupped his hand about his mouth and cried urgently, 'Stand to everybody. There's trouble coming our way.'

It was.

Suddenly, startlingly, a great ugly shape came rushing in out of the night sky some hundred yards away. It hit the ground in a great flurry of sand. It seemed to slither to the right, but the pilot caught it immediately. At a 100mph it raced across the floor of the desert, trailing a crazy wake of sand and stones behind. Then it hit a boulder and bounced a good twenty feet into the air once more. Yet again the pilot caught the glider and it came down, slowing down now, as he applied the brakes and the barbed wire wrapped round its skids snapped and burst like twine. Swaying and shaking as if it might fall apart at any moment, one wing splintering like matchwood as it struck a palm, it slithered to a crazy standstill in a thick cloud of dust.

For one long moment no one moved. Then the door of the glider flew off. Steele snapped out of his trance, as men in rimless helmets and camouflaged smocks started to pour of the glider, 'Let 'em have it,' he yelled. 'Fire at will!'

The watchers needed no urging. They knew they mustn't give the invaders from

141

the sky a chance to get under cover. What happened next was not war, but murder—the sheer pitiless massacre of the totally surprised Germans.

A wall of fire met them. Tracer zipped towards the open door in white fury. Germans went down everywhere. Stunned and confused by this lethal welcome, by this terrible thing happening to them, they went down screaming and crying, legs and arms flailing, as they were hit over and over again, piling up in front of the door like logs. A few retreated into the plane again, but its thin canvas was no proof against that deadly fire. In an instant it was riddled and torn to shreds and they could hear the muffled screams and moans of those dying inside the battered glider.

'Sanitäter,' someone called weakly from the bloody mess of dead and dying. But no stretcher bearer would be coming to the aid of the Germans this night.

Carried away by the crazy unreasoning blood lust of battle, Smith 175 seized two grenades from the dashboard of the LRDG's Dodge and doubled forward, crouched low.

'Hey, pack up yer bloody fool!' his mate Dawson yelled in alarm. But Smith 175 wasn't listening this terrible night. A German, who had probably cut his way through the fuselage at the other side of the ruined plane came from under the wing, machine pistol raised. He saw the running figure and fired a burst. Smith 175 zigzagged from side to side. The burst missed.

In the British positions someone screamed shrilly. Then Smith 175 flung the first of his grenades. It hit the ground just in front of the lone German. It exploded in a great burst of angry flame. Shards of steel flew everywhere. When the flame vanished, the lone German was lying, crumpled, on the ground. Slowly his severed head, still with the helmet on it, rolled away like a football abandoned by some careless child.

With the last of his strength, Smith 175 flung the other grenade through the open door of the glider and dropped to the ground, gasping for breath, lungs seemingly about to burst.

Next instant. *Crunch*. The canvas fuselage billowed in and out for a moment. Next moment it burst altogether and went up in flames. The firing stopped abruptly.

'Cease firing,' Steele yelled, 'Cease firing, do you hear!' The volleys gave way to spluttering single shots and then stopped altogether. A long echoing silence followed, broken only by the soft moaning of one of the dying Germans.

'Report any casualties, if you would, Stirling,' Steele commanded, not taking his gaze off the scene of bloody destruction and carnage. He had seen enough of war over the last three years, but never bodies stacked up like this.

A few minutes later Stirling came striding back. 'One casualty, Major,' he announced, 'Fatal.'

'One of your chaps or mine?'

'Neither,' Stirling answered. 'It was the Egyptian.'

'Dammit! ' Steele exclaimed. 'Now we'll never find out what's going on.'

'We know enough, though,' Stirling snapped. 'There can be only one Gippo of general rank on liaison at 8th Army HQ and we know about the wife too, thanks to young Bill here—'

There was a hollow ring and clatter, an obscene belch. Next moment a mortar bomb came hurtling out of the sky. A flash of ugly red flame. Suddenly a steaming brown hole opened in the desert yards away from their positions in the wadi like the work of some giant mole.

'Take cover,' Steele cried, as in the darkness whistles were shrilled and officers cried orders. 'It's the other glider!'

Suddenly they saw them coming out of the night. Little groups of infantry firing from the hip as they ran forward shouting

144

like men demented.

O'Sullivan took aim at an officer out in front, a tall skinny youngster with the gleam of the Iron Cross on his breast. As the defenders' first murderous volley crashed into the charging men, O'Sullivan fired. The young officer staggered. Frantically he clutched at his chest. Slowly, his legs buckled beneath him like those of a newborn calf. His pistol dropped from suddenly nerveless fingers. Then he went down and the steam started to go from the German attack. They started to pull back, firing as they did so, leaving half a dozen of their comrades dead or dying on the sand in front of the British positions.

For a little while there was a lull in the fighting, while the enemy re-grouped. Then the mortar belched fire once more and a line of sudden holes appeared the length of the British position. Snipers who had sneaked forward, worming their way through the darkness on their stomachs, began firing from the flanks, while a heavy machine gun, to the centre of the German positions, began hammering away. Morse zipped lethally through the darkness.

The defenders started to take casualties and Stirling crouched low with Steele, said grimly, 'If they rush us again, we'd see them off. But if they keep this up till

145

daybreak, then they'll whistle up the dive-bombers and it'll be nip-and-tuck whether we'll get out of this intact.'

'Agreed, Stirling,' said a worried Steele, who was bleeding from the forehead where he had been hit by a splinter, 'we've got to get out of here before first light. But as you know it's a dicey business trying to break off an action with the enemy so close. Besides we don't know if all the vehicles will start up at first go.'

'Sir.'

'O'Sullivan. All right, Bill what is it?' They all ducked as a sniper's bullet hit a boulder only feet away and showered them with bits of rock.

'Me, Smith 175 and Dawson here could hold them, while you pulled back to the vehicles. Once you started up, we'd bolt for it to the trucks.'

Steele considered it for a few moments, but when yet another man yelled out that he had been hit, he made his decision. 'Good for you, Bill. All right you're on your own. Give us at the most ten minutes. As soon as you spot a red signal flare, run for it. We'll be waiting for you. Good luck.'

Now they started to pull back, one by one, gliding away in the shadows while those who remained behind increased the volume of their fire to make the Germans believe the same number of men were in their positions.

Dawson and Smith 175 had taken over sten guns from two of the men who had stolen away into the shadows. Now as the last of the party vanished towards the trucks, they clipped on fresh magazines and took up the challenge.

But the Germans must have suspected a trick. For even above the noisy snap-and-crackle of the small arms battle, the noise of the motors in the wadi below could be heard. Suddenly a red flare shot into the sky followed an instant later by a green one, bathing the battle-ground in its eerie glowing light. It was the German signal for attack.

'Here they come!' O'Sullivan yelled frantically. 'Come on lads, pour it into them!'

'Up Guards and at 'em!' Smith 175 chuckled crazily and began firing.

'*Alles für Deutschland...alles für der Führer.*' Screaming hysterically, as if they were drugged or drunk, or perhaps both, the attackers streamed forward towards the three lone men in their holes. In front their officers blew whistles shrilly and fired their *Schmeissers* from the hip. Behind them the NCOs swore and threatened in red-faced anger, forcing the men to go on although

147

they were already taking casualties.

'Hold 'em!' O'Sullivan cried desperately. 'For Chrissake, *hold 'em!*'

They did... The three defenders stopped them at just fifty yards away. Many of the assault force were dead or wounded, sprawled out in hopeless abandon in the sand or writhing and twitching in their mortal agony. But there were enough of them going to ground just opposite to tell O'Sullivan that they didn't stand a chance when the Germans attacked again.

He flung a frantic look behind him to where the others were frantically attempting to get their vehicles started for the escape. No red flare, he told himself desperately. He made his decision, 'All right, lads,' he raised his voice above the ping-ping of the snipers' bullets which were striking the rocks angrily all around their positions. Knowing that the Germans opposite might understand conventional English, he ordered, 'Brigade of Guards will advance—to the rear—*now!*'

They got it. One moment later the three of them were running for all they were worth, bullets stitching the ground all around their flying heels...

Chapter Six

Dawn.

They huddled miserably over the first brew up of the new day, sipping the scalding hot tea. They were weary, unshaven, and definitely apprehensive, for even the most stupid of them knew that the mission they would soon embark on was compromised.

'There's no bloody use kidding ourselves,' Paddy Mayne said angrily, as he crouched next to the glowing petrol can over which they had brewed the tea, 'The Huns know what we're about. They wouldn't have gone to all that effort if they hadn't know what we planned. A squadron of precious bombers and then those glider-borne troops last night.' He shook his big head. 'We're walking into a trap, gentlemen.'

Steele stubbed out his cigarette almost angrily and said, 'I'm inclined to agree with you, Paddy.'

Stirling looked up from his big chipped mug, the steam wrcathing his face, and said, 'But we've *got* to make the attempt. If we don't, what will happen to the SAS?'

O'Sullivan sitting next to him stared across at Paddy Mayne. He was the weather vane of the little unit. He was the one who always was first to register any change. He did now. 'It's all right to talk like that, David,' Paddy snapped. 'But you've got to think of men's lives as well. We can't chuck 'em away—just like that.' He snapped two fingers like hairy pork sausages angrily. He glared at his superior officer.

Stirling opened his mouth to retort, but Steele beat him to it. He said hastily, 'At zero seven hundred I shall contact GHQ and put the case to them. I'll give them all the information we possess, including what Nouri told us about the Gippo general at 8th Army HQ. Then it's up to them to make the decisions. What do you say to that, gentlemen?'

There was a murmur of agreement, though it wasn't very enthusiastic on Stirling's part.

Ten yards away, watching them, Smith 175, a dewdrop hanging from the end of his pinched red nose, said, 'Dawsie, old pal, I think the officers an' gents ain't too happy with themselves this morning.'

Dawson, for his part, half closed his right eye in what he took to be a sage look, and commented, 'Officers and gents have problems the like of which you and

150

me common soldiers don't understand.'

Scornfully Smith 175 held up his middle finger.

Dawson wasn't offended. He said, 'Can't, old mucker, I've got a double decker bus up there already...'

Auchinleck stared at the signal from the LRDG, a frown on his long haggard face. Its arrival at GHQ had caused consternation. Immediately a message had been flashed to 8th Army HQ to have the Egyptian Army liaison officer, General Neguib, arrested. Field Security officers had been dispatched to the island on the Nile to arrest his wife, Yvonne, too. They had found her in bed with a middle aged Intelligence officer from Auchinleck's own staff, who to everyone's surprise, was wearing a pair of her frilly French lace knickers.

But the details of Egyptian Army treachery and espionage didn't concern Auchinleck now, as he sat ramrod-straight in his chair under the whirling ceiling fan, which merely stirred the warm air in his office. His preoccupation was with the projected Rommel raid. He knew just how much Churchill was for it and he knew, too, that his own position was very precarious now that his last offensive in the desert had failed. It wouldn't take much more for Churchill to fire him, he told himself.

All the same, he didn't want to risk the valuable young lives of such brave men as Keyes and Stirling and their subordinates for nothing. He passed a big hand across his furrowed brow a little wearily. Of course, it was the duty of a commander to send his men to what the commander knew was certain death if he felt the risk was worthwhile. But was it now?

Auchinleck knew he was risking his career, but he couldn't bring it upon himself to make the correct decision under the existing circumstances. The man who dreamed up the assassination plan in the first place would have to do that. He pressed the bell on his desk. His military secretary appeared at once, as if he had been waiting beyond the door all the time, pad already in his hand. 'Sir?'

'Make a signal, Jackson,' Auchinleck ordered.

'To whom, sir?'

'To the Right Honourable Winston S. Churchill...'

Churchill, clad only in a short silk vest which barely covered his rotund belly, but already with a big cigar clasped between his teethless gums, passed the signal to the Chief-of-the-Imperial-General-Staff

152

and growled, 'Well, what do you make of it, Alanbrooke?'

The dour Ulsterman read the signal and said after a few moments, 'Obviously he's leaving the decision to you, Prime Minister.'

'Exactly,' Churchill said, dipping the end of his cigar in the glass of brandy that stood on his night table. 'Why the devil do you have generals who can't make decisions for themselves, Alanbrooke?' he asked accusingly.

'Because, Prime Minister, you're always interfering when they do—always looking over their shoulders.'

Churchill gave him a toothless grin. 'You don't mince your words, Field Marshal,' he lisped.

Alanbrooke made no comment. He waited in grim silence, no emotion on his wrinkled, hook-nosed face. He knew already that Churchill would make the decision for the 'Auk'. It was out of his hands.

Churchill sucked at his cigar thoughtfully. 'I know you dislike this whole Rommel business, Alanbrooke. But I can see no other alternative. If your soldiers can't defeat him in the field, then we must find another way of dealing with him.'

Alanbrooke's craggy face flushed a little. 'The Germans, sir, have better tanks and better guns than we have. There is nothing wrong with the British soldier, sir,' he added hotly. 'It is just that he doesn't have the right equipment and the right leaders.'

'Sack them, then,' Churchill retorted in no way offended by the cold fury of Alanbrooke's words.

'Who should I put in their place?' Alanbrooke snapped back. 'Our generals are all pretty much the same. They have been used to fighting small colonial wars for most of their careers. Now they are fighting against a top professional general commanding a mainly European army. It is a totally different business. Different type of leadership, different type of tactics, different type of strategy.'

'Spare me the lecture, Alanbrooke,' Churchill said without a trace of anger in his voice. As always Churchill simply did not listen to objections. He rode over them roughshod. 'Rommel must be gotten rid of. There are no two ways about it. If they can't kidnap him, they must kill him.' He scratched his genitals idly, puffing away at the big cigar as he did so.

Alanbrooke's frown of disapproval deepened. He told himself this wasn't the way to conduct a war. You didn't murder the enemy general just because you couldn't beat him. 'So you're planning to go ahead

154

with this business, Prime Minister?' he asked.

'Yes.' Churchill's voice was suddenly harsh. 'I shall take full responsibility. And there is no need for you to look so disapproving, Alanbrooke. So far this war has been for the British Empire solely one defeat after another. There is no respect for us anywhere, neither in the enemy camp, nor in that of the neutral countries. Even our cousins across the sea, the Americans, feel we are performing poorly. With this Rommel business we shall show them all that we can be quite as efficient and as ruthless as the Huns.'

Alanbrooke shrugged slightly. 'Then so be it, sir. You have made your mind up.'

'I have. I shall signal Auchinleck this very morning.' He grunted and pulled the vest over his head to reveal his hairless, very white, pot-bellied body. 'Now I shall go and have my bath.' Puffing happily he waddled out into the next room, leaving the Field Marshal to stare at his fleshy buttocks in despair...

Keyes looked up at the signals officer who had just brought in the decode from GHQ in triumph. 'So it's on after all, Jenkins. Jolly good show!'

Jenkins answered stolidly, 'Looks like it, sir. We've heard from the Navy, in Alex as well, sir. They're standing by for us. According to their liaison chappie, they are standing by to sail within the next forty-eight hours.'

'Excellent, excellent,' Keyes said enthusiastically. 'It's all working out to plan. Thank you, Jenkins, you can go. ' He bent down to his papers once more, mind racing with the things he had to do over the next forty-eight hours.

As soon as Jenkins had gone, however, his eyes were directed at his own image in the mirror on the far wall of his office. Outside a sergeant in charge of bayonet practise was bellowing, 'Go on, Horrocks, stick it into 'im...right in the guts...that's the stuff... Now twist the frigging thing free and let him have the butt under his jaw... That's the style. Bags o' blood.'

But Keyes did not hear the raucous voice and the wild cries of the commandos charging forward at the dummies. He saw only himself, heard only his inner voices. Nearly twenty-five years before, his father had made his name in that great raid on Zeebrugge in 1918. It had brought him fame and, if not fortune, at least great honour. Now here he was at twenty-four in charge of his own battalion, ready to carry out another raid, just like his father, the admiral, had done before him. It, too, could bring him the fame and honours he craved. *But what if it fails?* an inner voice queried.

'It won't fail,' he answered firmly, talking aloud to himself in the manner of lonely men, staring at his own face in the mirror, 'because I won't let it...'

Chapter Seven

'Dear Elizabeth,' Keyes wrote, as outside sailors lugged stores to the submarine, while others winched aboard crates of ammunition they would perhaps need once they were ashore, 'just a few thoughts for you. Today is the three months' anniversary of my promotion to Lt. Col, which is a fantastic bit of luck at my age. I've collected a gong, too. It causes jealousy of course. For a major of forty-two in an office to see me walk in at twenty-four is like a red rag to a bull. I have met two of my instructors at Sandhurst, both majors, who looked pretty sideways at me.'

Outside he could hear the regular stamp of marching boots and an NCO bellowing, 'swing them arms now...bags o'swank, lads." Keynes paused a moment in his writing and nodded his approval.

That would be his commando volunteers arriving.

'To other matters, dearest Elizabeth,' he continued, 'I remember when this show was in its early stages, I told the Adj, 'If we get this job, Tommy, it's one people will remember us by.' Well, we've got it.

Naturally, although this letter probably won't be censored, unless there's a spot check, I can't tell you what the show is. All I can do is tell you to ask Dad what the 'Trafalgar Memorandum' is. The one the old chap wrote on October 9th, 1805. He'll know and then you can guess what I'm up to.'

He grinned and visualized the look on his father's face when his sister Elizabeth asked him what the 'Trafalgar Memorandum' was. He'd probably look up from his desk in the old dark pannelled study and bark, as if he were back on the quarter-deck, 'Why, my dear girl, I would have thought that everyone knew what the 'Trafalgar Memorandum' was. In part it states, that Nelson's captains must make every effort to capture the froggies' commander-in-chief—Villeneuve.'

Then, Keyes told himself happily, the old boy's jaw would drop and he would exclaim, 'Well, I'll be damned, Elizabeth. D'yer know what Geoffrey's up to?'

Elizabeth would shake her head in bewilderment and the old Admiral would snort, 'Why he's after Rommel himself, the young devil!'

Keyes' grin vanished. He added his signature with a flourish and sealed up the buff envelope. He scribbled his initials on the left hand corner with an air of finality; then left it on the desk to be picked up by the naval postal clerk. Now there was nothing more for him to do in Alexandria.

Putting on his balmoral adorned with the black hackle of the 11th Scottish Commando, he went outside, blinking in the sudden glare of the sun.

Over at the dock, the submarine which would take him to Libya, HMS *Torbay* was a hive of activity. Ratings scurried about everywhere. Cranes creaked and gave off great belches of steam, commandos stacked their weapons and placed the folboats the reconnaissance party on the beach would use on the quay ready for stowing. All seemed controlled chaos.

Keyes strolled over to his men. They attempted to stand to attention but he waved them to remain standing at ease. 'Won't be long now, lads,' he said cheerfully, proud of how fit and well they all looked.

All of them were volunteers and they

had volunteered for an operation which was still unknown to them. In the interest of security, they would be told what their objective was once the *Torbay* was way out at sea. 'I'd like to say one thing, chaps. This show is going to make the headlines, I can tell you that. If we pull it off—and I know we will—the commandos will be on the map at last.'

There was a spontaneous cheer and Keyes flushed with pleasure, in the same instant that the tough, determined-looking skipper of the *Torbay*, Lieutenant Commander Miers strode over to the soldiers, 'All right, Colonel Keyes, you can start embarking your brown jobs now.'

'Brown jobs, Miers?' Keyes queried, puzzled.

'That's what we call you chaps of the army,' Miers answered with a slight smile on his tough face. 'All right, let's get cracking.'

One hour later they were underway with the dazzling white skyline of Alexandria disappearing into the heat haze behind them. Cramped as they were in the dripping hull of the submarine, which smelled of diesel oil, urine and stale food, they were happy, lounging on the deck, playing 'housey-housey', trying to read in the weak yellow light or doing what

160

British soldiers always did in moments like this—snoring in happy oblivion.

Up near the conning tower, Miers explained to Keyes how the commandos would be landed. 'I'll dispatch you in two parties. First will go your recce chaps in the folboats. We're expecting choppy water and those boats are the very devil to launch, but we'll do our best.'

'I'm sure you will, Commander,' Keyes said, eyeing the green-glowing dials everywhere and wondering what they all were for. They looked damned complicated. 'Please carry on.'

'Then when the recce party signals the beach is clear, we'll dispatch the main party. I should think the whole operation might take two hours so we're going to do it during the hours of darkness. Too risky otherwise. There are plenty of small German and Italian installations near the landing beach.'

'Don't worry, Commander,' Keyes attempted to reassure the young submariner who already had won the DSO, a pretty high decoration for a youngster. 'My chaps are well trained in all kinds of seaborne disembarkations—'

'Sir,' it was a rating seated at a kind of a wheel with earphone pressed tightly to his cropped head.

'What it is, Jones?' Miers snapped, the

161

easy-going look vanished in an instant from his young face.

'I'm getting an echo, sir. And I don't think it's one of ours.'

Miers acted immediately. 'Ring for silent running,' he commanded urgently. 'We've just picked up a ship's propellers. Could be enemy.' He swung round on Keyes, 'Tell your chaps, Colonel to pipe down.

We shall now make as little noise as possible.'

The faces of Keyes' commandos blanched. None of them had been in a submarine before. Now the thought that above them there was possibly an enemy ship trying to sink them made even the toughest of them fearful.

Five minutes passed. Jones at the hydrophone tensed over his instrument, barking out depths and speeds every few seconds. 'Above us now, sir,' his voice suddenly lowered to a whisper. Faintly Keyes could hear the noise of ship's engines.

A series of metallic pings ran the length of the hull. Miers bit his bottom lip. 'They've located us,' he whispered to Keyes. Then to the man in front of him next to the periscope, 'Stop both, Number One.'

The other officer repeated the order softly. A moment later the whine of the electric motors which propelled the submarine under water ceased. Slowly the submarine slid to a halt.

Now they waited tensely in a blood-red light, for all other had been extinguished, their faces lathered in sweat, as if they were greased, staring mesmerized at the dripping steel hull above their heads, apprehensive.

There was another ripple of ping-pings along the metal casement. They signified that the enemy operators had latched onto them. A thrashing of the water by the enemy ship's screw, clearly audible to the tense silent, waiting men. A series of soft plops, 'Depth charges,' Miers said quietly.

Suddenly, startlingly, the *Torbay* was buffeted from side to side by mighty punches as if from a pair of gigantic fists. The glass of the instruments shattered under the impact. In the little galley, the mugs fell from their hooks and smashed to the deck. Here and there plates buckled. Seawater started to seep in. One of the commandos, his face distorted by fear, cried out. Keyes flashed him a sharp look. He clapped a hand to his mouth to stifle any more cries of fear.

The noise of the enemy ship's screws started to grow quieter. Keyes' face must have betrayed his sense of relief. Miers, his own features very grave, mouthed the words silently. 'Not yet. They'll be back.'

163

They waited tensely, each man frozen in position like figures in some ghastly tableau. Only the fear and apprehension in each individual's eyes showed that they were human.

Again that dreaded series of pings ran the length of the hull. The screws of the enemy ship thundered once more. They were followed an instant later by the dull thuds of the great one ton depth charges hitting the water as they fell from the stern of the enemy craft.

Keyes found himself digging his fingernails cruelly into the palms of his hands. His breath was coming in shallow gasps. His whole body was rigid with tension. He felt no fear, just a sense of hopelessness, despair that he couldn't fight back in this strange undersea battle.

The first depth charge struck a great hammer blow against the hull of the submarine. The *Torbay* lurched. Hurriedly Keyes grabbed a stanchion and hung there panting urgently. The second depth charge exploded close by. The submarine shook and rattled. Plates sprung open everywhere. Water started to pour in. Some of the commandos, fear written all over their faces, which were coloured an unreal red hue in the light, sprang to their feet. Hastily Keyes hissed, 'Stand fast there. Get down again.'

They swallowed but obeyed.

Another gigantic hammer blow against the hull. The *Torbay* tilted at a crazy angle and it sank. Hastily Number One called out the depth as the helmsman, sweating furiously and cursing under his breath tried to right the boat.

Then the enemy craft started to pull away again and the hydrophone operator called his findings. Miers sprang into action. 'Torpedo mates. Get the fish out of the bow. We'll try an old trick on them. They might buy it.'

As the soldiers gaped, not knowing what was going on, four petty officers hurried through the crowded sub and started opening the great steel tube which held the torpedo.

Miers turned to his Number One again, 'Number One, some old duds, a couple of loaves of bread—and as much fuel oil as we can spare.'

'Ay ay, sir,' the young second-in-command said, not questioning the strange order for a moment.

'What's going on?' Keyes asked in bewilderment.

His eyes fixed on the men labouring to get the big 'fish', the one ton torpedo out of its tube, their singlets stained black with sweat. Miers said over his shoulder, 'It's an old trick. Won't work on an experienced

165

destroyer skipper. With luck though it might on this one. The Huns are only too eager to report a kill even if they haven't had one.'

Another depth charge exploded close by. The lights went out for a moment and someone yelled out in panic. Christ, Keyes thought, now we've had it. But in a moment the red lights flickered on again and they could see that the boat had sprung even more plates. Now the water was up their ankles.

Miers didn't seem to notice. He cried, as the sweating petty officers finally lowered the torpedo out of the tube, 'All right, leave the fish. Number One, put on the duds and stuff.'

Hastily the overalls and singlets were stuffed in the empty torpedo tube. Oil followed. Hastily the door was shut and locked.

'Stand by to fire, Number One,' Miers ordered.

'All right, torpedo mate. Fire,' the younger officer commanded.

There was a rush of compressed air, the faint sound of bubbles of trapped air heading for the surface and then they froze, waiting, each man wrapped up in a cocoon of his own hopes and fears, to see if their trick had worked.

All eyes were now directed at the

hydrophone operator, as he sat on his leather stool, earphones pressed to his ears, as if his very life depended upon it. What was he going to report? Had the enemy been fooled?

The minutes ticked by leadenly. Now, even when they strained, they could not hear the noise of the enemy's screws. Keyes opened his mouth to say, 'We've done it.' But Miers stopped him before he could speak. 'Give it time,' he mouthed the words carefully. 'Let's not rush it.'

Thirty minutes became an hour. Still Miers did not move. He had been through this all before. Once he had stuck it out for eighteen hours below the surface until the crew were dying from lack of oxygen where they lay. Inside the battered submarine, loaves, tins, cracked photos slopped back and forth in the seawater which had now risen to their knees. The stench was terrible.

At one and a half hours, Miers forced a smile and whispered, 'And no more farting everybody. There's enough bloody gas down here as it is.' His sally roused not a smile. They were all too exhausted. Here and there a man started to gasp a little hectically, his chest heaving swiftly, as if he were already choking for breath...

At two hours, the men beginning to cough and choke now as the seawater got to the deadly chemicals of their electric batteries and poisonous gas started to seep into the interior, Miers whispered to the hydrophone operator, 'Anything?'

The rating, face pale with fatigue, shook his head. 'Nothing for well over an hour, sir.'

Slowly, infinitely, slowly, as if it was taking him all his willpower to rise, Miers got up and struggled over to the periscope. 'Up scope,' he ordered.

As the gleaming steel tube slid upwards, he tilted his cap back to front and peered into the calibrated glass, turning up the intensifier to catch every last little bit of light. Carefully, he swung the instrument round a full 360 degrees, taking his time, knowing that if he slipped up now, it might well mean the end of the *Torbay*.

Finally he turned and ordered his Number One to the periscope, saying in a broken voice, as if finding the words was difficult, 'I think they've gone for good.'

There was a ragged weak cheer from the commandos and Miers turned to his Number One and said, 'Take her up, will you?'

Moments later fresh sea air was flushing out the stifling fetid stench of the interior of the submarine and the men were sucking great mouthfuls of it gratefully. 'Well,' Miers said a little wearily, 'we seem to

168

have got out of that little mess nicely. Let's hope the next three days, till we reach our objective, pass without incident.'

Keyes smiled. 'Amen to that,' he said. 'But I'll tell you one thing, Commander, I never want to see the inside of a sub again. Next time I'll walk.'

But there would never be a next time for Lt. Colonel Geoffrey Keyes.

Chapter Eight

'We've got our marching orders,' Stirling announced and sat down with the little group of officers watching Smith 175 fry his celebrated corned beef fritters and chipped tinned potatoes.

Smith 175 was saying, 'If anyone offers me another slice of bully beef after the war, gentlemen, I'll strangle him. Still the old corned beef fritters aren't so bad.'

With his bayonet he turned them over carefully in a blackened frying pan and dropped a little more margarine into it.

Stirling nodded his approval and continued, 'We're to move out with Steele's boys at zero one hundred hours. We'll march till first light and then lie low during the day. The same thing the following night. We should be in position at dawn on the fifteenth, Thursday, if I remember correctly.'

O'Sullivan, huddled in a greatcoat for it was still quite cold smiled softly. In the desert he could never remember, too, what time it was. There were no morning papers, regular hours, even regular three meals a day by which a person could calculate the passage of time. Days, weeks, months meant nothing when you were 'up the blue', save when the time for a leave in Cairo or Alexandria approached, then a soldier started to take notice of the days.

For a moment he thought of that last brief leave and Yvonne. Now he knew why she had sobbed in the middle of the night. She might have been a tart, but she had had feelings. She had not quite liked all she had been forced to do. He wondered where she was right at this moment, then he dismissed the thought and concentrated on listening to Stirling.

The latter was saying, 'Now as Paddy here has said, it appears that we are only to play a back-up role, a kind of flank guard to Keyes' commandos.' He winked solemnly. 'But there's many a slip between the cup and the lip. Once the LRDG boys have left, to ride to their rendezvous position, there's nothing to say that we shouldn't march a little closer to

170

where the action is going to take place. You've all memorized the layout of Beda Littoria. Therefore, you know where the two barracks are, Rommel's HQ and his private quarters.' Stirling lowered his voice, as if he thought he might be overheard. 'Now there will be nobody to stop us taking up our positions slightly south of those installations. Then when the balloon goes up, we're not mere spectators but actors.'

Paddy Mayne's face lit up, 'By Jesus,' he cried and made Smith 175 almost drop the blackened frying pan. 'Now you're talking, David.'

'Sir,' Smith 175 said in a pained voice, 'you nearly made me upset breakfast.'

'Bugger breakfast!' Paddy answered without rancour, 'Go on, David, tell us more.'

'I think with a bit of care we'll be able to avoid casualties through friendly fire. All of us know the sound difference between our own weapons and those of the Huns. So that's no problem.'

'Keyes is though,' Paddy Mayne objected, his smile suddenly vanishing. 'He won't like it one bit. He wants this show all to himself, you know, David.'

'Well, hard luck on him. The commandos have had their chance since they were formed last year, and they haven't

171

made much of it. Now it's the turn of the Special Air Service.'

Listening attentively now, O'Sullivan told himself that he was learning—slowly admittedly—a new side of the war. Regular soldiers like Keyes and Stirling, too, weren't only fighting the war; they were fighting each other as well. Understandably so, for war was their great chance to build their own little empires, achieve the kind of rank in a few short years—if they lived—which would take a lifetime in times of peace. Yet, it seemed to him, that this shouldn't be so. The real and sole purpose of the war should be for the soldier to defeat the enemy. There should be no other considerations.

'We'll draw up the new plan and inform the chaps this morning,' Stirling said. Stirling continued, 'This afternoon we'll get kitted up and have some shut-eye. We'll set off as soon as it's dark and—'

'Is it convenient to serve breakfast now, sir?' Smith 175 butted in, in the grave tones of some ancient family retainer, 'I prefer not to overdo the fritters and the potato chips are a really lovely brown colour.'

O'Sullivan grinned at the solemn guardsman who was so proud of his primitive cooking, as if he were some great French gourmet chef. Paddy Mayne grinned too.

'Put a sock in it, Smithie,' he chortled. 'Dish out the fodder. I'm starving.'

But Paddy Mayne and the rest of the officers were not destined to enjoy much of Smith 175's celebrated bully beef fritters. O'Sullivan had just dug his fork into the steaming hot fritter, breaking through the batter to the bright red meat beneath, under the benign gaze of the proud cook, when the lookout on the rocks of the wadi above cupped his hands about his mouth and shouted, 'Visitors, gentlemen.'

O'Sullivan and the others dropped their forks as if they were red hot. Breakfast was forgotten immediately for there were no British troops within a hundred miles of this remote place. The 'visitors' could only be either nomadic Arabs or the enemy.

Hurriedly Stirling made his dispositions, as without orders the SAS troopers took up their defensive positions. 'Runner,' he called, 'get over that hill to Major Steele and tell him we've sighted someone. Paddy you take charge down here. Bill, you come with me and we'll have a look-see. Smithie dowse the flames.'

For a moment a crestfallen Smith 175 looked as if he might disobey Stirling's order. Then grumbling to himself about 'nobody cares about the frigging trouble I take,' he started to heap sand over the flickering blue petrol flame.

173

Stirling and O'Sullivan threw themselves onto the rock next to the lookout, making themselves as small as possible. 'Over there at three o'clock, sir,' the lookout whispered.

Hastily the two of them raised their glasses, shading the lenses with one hand so that there would be no light reflected from them. A long line of plodding swaying camels slid into the circles of gleaming glass. On each a soldier bounced up and down, clinging to the beasts' humps carefully. Up front there was a single white horse. On it sat, erect and proud, a white silk cape fluttering from his shoulders, the detachment's commander, and unlike the rank-and-file he was white. 'Italians, I imagine,' Stirling hissed. 'The Italian camel corps out on patrol.'

'They're pretty deep into the desert,' O'Sullivan said.

'I know, Bill. The Huns never go this far. They're obviously using the wops as a flank guard—'

'What is it?' O'Sullivan asked sharply.

'Dammit,' Stirling replied, 'I think they're changing direction. Look they're coming our way.'

O'Sullivan focused his glasses on the officer. He had risen in his spurs and with a dramatic gesture of his riding crop, he had indicated southwards. Obediently his Arab rank-and-file jerked the heads of their beasts round and started to follow him deeper into the desert.

'That's torn it, sir,' Dawson, the lookout said, 'Once they come level, they'll spot the jeeps and the Dodges. We ain't that well camouflaged.'

'I know,' Stirling snapped a little angrily, 'You don't have to rub it in, Guardsman.'

'Sorry, sir.'

'What's the drill?' O'Sullivan asked urgently, lowering his glasses. Obviously the Italian patrol didn't suspect anything —yet. But once they spotted the vehicles here way out in the desert where there were no Germans, they wouldn't need a crystal ball to know that they belonged to their enemies.

Stirling seemed able to read the younger officer's mind, for he said, 'If they pass us without spotting us, well and good, Bill. If they don't,' he shrugged. 'Then there cannot be any survivors.'

O'Sullivan looked at Stirling, face aghast. 'You mean kill the lot.'

Stirling nodded grimly. 'We're going on an op. We can't be bothered with prisoners. We're short of men as it is. Can't spare any to guard prisoners.' He made a significant cutting gesture with his forefinger along the length of his neck. 'No two ways about it. All right, let's get

175

back to the others. Make our dispositions.' Without waiting to see if O'Sullivan was following, he started to slither down the rocks back into the wadi.

Dawson looked at the young officer and saw the shock still in his face. He told himself not unkindly, 'Brave but still wet behind the lugs. He's got some learning to do before this frigging war is over.' Then O'Sullivan was gone too.

Now the watchers could see the riders quite easily. The long column of mounted men were riding into the sun so that they were half blinded by its glare. But the men lying tensely in the sand were at no such a disadvantage. They saw the riders clearly enough to note the dark, hook-nosed faces of the Arabs and a whiter, handsome, somewhat foppish face of their officer.

'Looks like a nancy boy to me, sir,' Smith 175 grunted as he tugged the butt of the bren gun more firmly into his shoulder, squinting along the barrel as he did so.

'He can be anything he likes,' O'Sullivan answered in a whisper, 'as long as he doesn't spot us. If he does—' he didn't finish the rest of the sentence. He couldn't.

Now the riders were some five hundred yards away, moving at the slow pace of the camels. Too slow, O'Sullivan thought. It gave the riders far too much time to survey the desert floor, though in the wadi, they were slightly below that level. With luck the Italian patrol might just pass them by without noticing the men hidden there.

But the enemy's luck had run out on this hot Tuesday morning in the middle years of the war. Suddenly the elegant officer in his white cloak gestured imperiously with his stick. *'Bollocks,'* Smith 175 swore, 'they're coming our way!'

They were. At the trot, his elegantly breeched bottom going up and down in the glistening saddle, the officer led the way, with the clumsy camel riders following him.

'Stand to!' Sterling hissed.

The men squinted down the barrels of their weapons, knowing that in a minute the fun and games would start. 'Come on into my parlour, the spider said to the fly,' Paddy Mayne chuckled gleefully. He had no inhibitions about the slaughter to come. They were the enemy. They deserved to die.

Now they were only two hundred yards away. In a couple of minutes they'll spot us. O'Sullivan told himself grimly.

Suddenly, the young Italian officer tugged sharply at the bit of his white stallion. It reared up, forelegs flailing the air, while the Italian pointed his stock and yelled something in Arabic.

'Fire,' Stirling yelled urgently.

The first volley caught the riders completely by surprise. The officer flew over the head of his mount, as it went down on its forelegs whinnying piteously, a sudden scarlet stain spreading over its white shoulder. The officer pulled himself up and attempted to reach for his revolver. He never made it. Smith 175 swung the bren gun round. His next burst stitched a line of red buttonholes the length of the officer's elegant tunic. He went down howling with pain, writhed in the sand for a moment, thrashing it with his highly polished riding boots.

Now here and there the Arabs were throwing away their weapons and holding up their arms in surrender, wailing and calling upon Allah to save them. But on this cruel burning morning Allah took no heed. Relentlessly the SAS men continued firing until the desert floor lay littered with the bodies of the Arabs like bundles of abandoned rags, save for one.

Wounded though he was, he dug his heels into the side of his beast frantically, and tugging at the rein, brought the camel round. Slumped as if he might fall off at any moment, he set the camel off racing away.

'Knock the bugger out of the saddle!' Paddy Mayne yelled and springing to his feet started pumping shot after shot at the fleeing Arab. To no avail. The wounded rider disappeared into the distance and in the end Paddy Mayne realized it served no purpose to fire anymore.

Numbly they stared at the dead and dying camel corps men lying out there in the sand, with flies already beginning to descend upon them, buzzing greedily around their sightless eyes, creeping into their nostrils so that in an instant their dead faces were covered in a moving, crawling blue-black.

Smith 175 sniffed and wiped the sweat from his forehead. 'That's put the mopers on it,' he said to no one in particular. 'First them Jerries at the oasis and now this little lot. I hope none of us is taken prisoner. Don't think he'll live long.' With that he slung his bren gun over his shoulder and plodded back to where his celebrated bully beef fritters were cooling in the mess tins.

Chapter Nine

Churchill was in high good humour. He had come from the afternoon session of the House, where he had turned a motion of censure against the government on account of the handling of the recent

British offensive in the Western Desert into a personal triumph for himself. In the end only three members of the House had voted against the overwhelming number of MPs who had voted in the government's favour.

Thereafter he had had a splendid dinner with several members of his cabinet in his underground 'war room' in Whitehall, where he had consumed a considerable amount of good claret and brandy. He had revealed to them what was afoot in the Western Desert at that very moment and when that 'mealy-mouthed bugger' Morrison, his Labour Home Secretary, had objected—why the man had been a 'conchie' in the last show—on moral grounds.

Churchill had thundered, 'Last year I stated publicly that if Hitler invaded Hell itself, I would say a good word for the Devil himself, if needs be. Didn't I this very summer declare myself the loyal ally of that Soviet monster Stalin, after Hitler had invaded his thrice-accursed country—that after I had been fighting against his regime for over a quarter of a century? Gentlemen', he had growled in that familiar voice of his which was known throughout the civilized world, 'in wartime, morality must be tossed out of the window *tout de suite.*'

He had eyed the weedy, bespectacled

180

Home Secretary like the Chinese God of Plenty suffering from bellyache, stabbing his big cigar at him like an offensive weapon, and it had concluded with, 'So now I have my own bunch of hired killers in the Western Desert!' He had shrugged his fat shoulders carelessly. 'What of it, gentlemen?'

That had silenced them and now he sat in his panelled study at Chequers, replete and happy, knowing that he was in complete charge of the embattled British Empire. The only danger that threatened him was another defeat in the Western Desert. If that happened, then his enemies, and he knew he had plenty even within his own party, would bring out the long knives. He had no illusions about that.

The elderly maid scampered in and silently started to draw the blackout curtains. He didn't seem to notice, but then he never seemed to notice servants. Then he appeared to do so and said, 'When you are finished, please send in Mr Colville. I know he's leaving for the Royal Air Force tonight.'

'Yes, sir.' The maid curtseyed and creaked out.

Colville, Churchill's private secretary, dark and elegant, came in almost immediately, holding in his hand a signal, bearing the words 'Most Secret'.

'Well, you're off by the six o'clock train,' Churchill said. 'How old are you?'

'Twenty-six,' Colville replied.

'At twenty-six Napoleon commanded the armies of Italy,' Churchill snorted with a cheeky grin.

'Pitt was Prime Minister at twenty-four.' Colville retorted, equally cheekily.

'On that score you win,' the 60-year-old Premier conceded.

'I'll bring one last signal for you, Prime Minister,' Colville retorted, realizing he had bested the PM at repartee—a very rare event. 'And I think it will please you, sir.'

Churchill almost snatched it from his hand.

Swiftly he read through the signal from Auchinleck, then he looked up at his former secretary in triumph. 'It is indeed good news.' He puffed out his chest, one hand inside his breast as if he might well be about to make a speech to the House. 'The stage is set,' he declared. 'The actors are in place. The drama can commence.'

Colville nodded sombrely. But how many of those 'actors' would survive the 'drama' he asked himself. But there was no answer—yet—to that overwhelming question...

PART THREE

Kill Rommel

'It's no good fart-arsing about shooting German private soldiers. That's not the way to win the war. Go for the top. Chop off the head and the body will wither away of its own accord.'

The Sayings of Paddy Mayne

Chapter One

'There they are,' Miers said urgently, as he and Keyes stood in the conning tower of the motionless submarine, peering into the inky gloom. 'Can you see, Colonel?'

Keyes, muffled up in his greatcoat against the night cold, strained his eyes even more. Then he saw it. Red followed white and then another white light. It was the signal agreed upon with the reconnaissance party four hours before. 'It's all clear,' he announced. 'The beach is OK.'

'Yes,' Miers agreed, very businesslike now. He knew that every minute the *Torbay* lay on the surface motionless this spelled danger for the submarine. 'Would you get your people ready, Colonel. I'd appreciate it if you could disembark as soon as possible.' He looked at the white slurry of water beating against the submarine's casement and added. 'The sea's running a swell. It's not going to be easy.'

'Yes, Commander,' Keyes agreed. 'My chaps are ready and we'll inflate as soon as we get the dinghies on deck. Ah, here comes the first one.' He nodded at the four dark shapes dragging with them the limp rubber case of the dinghy.

Half an hour later all four dinghies were inflated and the men waiting to board them hung on to the single wire running the length of the deck as the wind increased and the *Torbay* rocked in the swell. Miers nodded his approval. 'All right, Colonel, get your chaps into the dinghies. I'm going to submerge slightly and that will float the craft off and into the swell.' He held out his hand. 'Good luck, Colonel. I hope the next time you're in Alex, you'll let me buy you a couple of ice-cold *Rheingolds,*' he meant the well-known Egyptian beer.

'Of course,' Keyes said heartily seizing the young skipper's hand and shaking it. 'Let's say two weeks from now.'

Miers laughed. 'Well, I must say you're very confident Colonel.'

'Of course I am. The operation is going well and I have a grand bunch of chaps. I'm counting on that beer.'

'You shall have it,' Miers said, but Colonel Geoffrey Keyes would never sink another *Rheingold*.

Now they hung on, one hand on the wire above their heads, the other on the wet slippery side of the rubber dinghies, as the *Torbay's* diesels throbbed and she slowly began to sink. The water rose swirling around the sides of the frail craft. 'All right,' Keyes called softly, 'stand by to let go everybody.' He put his hand over the side. The ice-cold water was up to his wrist. It was deep enough. 'Let's go,' he commanded.

As one the commandos took their hands away from the single wire, immediately the boats were seized by the sea. They went over the side with a soft plop. Next instant the commandos were paddling furiously against the current, the dinghies being tossed up and down by the swell, as if they were children's toys.

Despite the night's coldness, Keyes found himself sweating in a flash, as he paddled with all his strength, trying with the rest to keep the dinghy heading in the general direction of the shore and that faint winking light being flashed by the reconnaissance party.

Yard by yard, rowing and paddling for all they were worth, their shoulder muscles red-hot and burning with the strain, the commandos directed their craft to the beach. Time seemed endless. They were tossed back over and over again. Then they would hurtle forward once more, plunging down into the troughs of the angry waves. An instant later they were propelled up onto the top of the waves, hanging there precariously for a terrifying moment before they plunged downwards yet once again.

'Keep it up, lads,' Keyes gasped, trying to encourage them. 'Not much further now.'

And in truth they were slowly approaching the landing beach. For in between the roar of the waves, Keyes could hear the slither and clattering of the shingle. Then they were coming in on the crest of a wave, driven forward at a tremendous rate. They hit the beach. The first dinghy overturned, turfing the men, coughing and spluttering into the icy-cold water.

One by one the dinghies made it, being hauled in by the reconnaissance party. Soaking wet and almost exhausted, Keyes reached into his pack with stiff frozen fingers. He dragged out the bottle and uncorked it and said, while the reconnaissance party set about lighting a bonfire in the shelter of a gully to dry the soaked commandos, 'Any needy cases? I've got a bottle of rum here for those who want it.'

That raised a weary laugh and so as the soaked men stood around the blazing fire of camel thorn, the steam rising from their uniforms so that they appeared to be wreathed in fog, the bottle was passed hastily from hand to hand.

There was only a thimbleful left for

Keyes. But it was enough. He felt the fiery rum burning down into his stomach and warmth flooded his chilled body. He gave the men another five minutes around the bonfire. Then he ordered, new energy soaring through his skinny body, 'All right, Sergeant Metcalfe, see that fire is put out. It's been going long enough.'

'Sir,' the big commando NCO snapped back and started pouring wet sand over the flames.

'Let's get the stores and personal kits sorted out, chaps,' Keyes continued. 'I've selected a wadi further inland. There are a few caves and ruined abandoned houses there, according to Intelligence. We'll lie up there for the night. All right, let's get cracking.'

Glad to be moving in that chill air, the commandos set to work with a will, gathering up the wooden crates of ammunition, grenades and high explosives, slinging their heavy packs over their shoulders.

Fifteen minutes later they were on their way to their hide-out, marching through the chill night under a cold star-studded velvet sky. They were on their way. Operation 'Kill Rommel' had commenced...

Forty miles away, the vehicles of the LRDG ground to a halt. Steele got out of the leading Dodge and walked across to where Stirling was standing, as stooped as ever, next to the first of the SAS's two jeeps. 'This is as far as we go, Stirling,' he said, keeping his voice low, for he knew that sound carried for miles across the desert at night time. 'I want to make the RV while it's still dark and lie up for the day. It seems to take longer and longer to get the vehicles satisfactorily camouflaged.'

'I understand,' Stirling answered, wishing that Steele would get on with it. He had some more ground to cover himself before first light, but he wasn't going to tell the LRDG commander that.

'Bit of final drill,' Steele went on, 'before we buzz off. We'll wait for four hours at the rendezvous point on Thursday. If you haven't made it by then with Keyes' Commandos, we'll move to point "X". You've got it marked on your map.'

Stirling nodded.

'There we'll wait another four hours on the following day. If you haven't made it by the end of those four hours then,' he shrugged and left the rest of his sentence unsaid.

Stirling knew what he meant though. If they hadn't made it by then, the LRDG group would give up on them and return to their base at the oasis. 'Fair enough,' he

190

said. 'I understand. No tickee, no washee sort of thing.'

'Exactly, Stirling.' Steele held out his hand. 'Best of luck, Stirling. Let's hope this op goes better for you SAS boys than the last one.'

'Thank you, Major. I'm sure it will,' the other man answered, taking the proferred hand. 'Soon the whole world's going to know what the SAS is about.'

In the icy light of the stars Steele looked slightly perplexed. But he said nothing and with a hasty goodbye, he walked back to the Dodge.

Paddy Mayne chuckled and said to O'Sullivan, whose head was buried in the thick collar of his greatcoat against the biting cold, 'Well said, David.'

'Do you really think that the SAS is going to be that famous?' O'Sullivan asked.

'Of course it is, m'boy,' Paddy said enthusiastically. 'Long after we're all dead, they'll still be talking about the SAS. We're the troops of the future. One day all armies'll have special forces like the SAS. David has started something which will make history. Now come on, let's stow our heavy gear in the jeep. We're going to walk, Bill.'

Following the two jeeps laden with their equipment, the little group of SAS troopers pressed on, moving ever closer to Beda Littorio. Up in front sitting next to Dawson, driving the lead jeep, Stirling was conscious that they were getting ever closer to Rommel's HQ—and that spelled out danger. For he was quite sure that the Desert Fox, as army commander, would be well guarded. Soon he knew he would have to find a hide-out for the morrow.

Stirling looked at the green-glowing dial of his wrist-watch. Zero four hundred hours. Perhaps two more hours before first light. Hastily he ran his mind over the position of the various installations of Rommel's headquarters area. It was pretty obvious it wouldn't be too healthy to position the men close to either of the two barracks when the balloon went up. Then he had it. The generator next to the second barracks. He could have the generator sabotaged in advance and cut the power lines. With the Jerries lacking communications, they'd be in like Flynn and do their bit before the Jerries had realized what had hit them.

Time passed. To the east the sky was starting to flush the first ugly white of the false dawn. Stirling peered ahead. In the new light he thought he could make out the silhouettes of buildings. Beda Littorio, he told himself and said to Dawson, 'Bear right, guardsman. Head for the last of those buildings, if you can see 'em?'

192

Dawson said, 'I can see 'em all right, sir.' He turned the wheel slightly and at the same snail's pace they started to head for the generator building.

Again time passed. Now they could see the buildings more clearly: a row of modernistic structures probably constructed by the Italians in the early thirties. Once their stucco exteriors had been brilliant white. But the war had taken its toll. Now the outside of the buildings was soiled and dirty.

Stirling ordered Dawson to stop the jeep. Behind it the men sat down. They needed the rest. Stirling focused his glasses. This was Beda Litorrio all right, he told himself. The layout was exactly as it had been on the Intelligence map. It was time they found cover and waited till the balloon went up.

Stirling selected a narrow gulley in which he thought they could lie up without being spotted from the nearest building, the generator one, some five hundred yards away. All the same, he wasn't leaving that to chance. As the two jeeps drove carefully into the narrow chasm, the rest of the troopers started to lay metal channels they used for getting out of sticky patches in the desert across the top of the gulley. Others filled them in with sand so that a cursory inspection would make the observer think that it was part of the desert floor. Finally, the weary troopers piled camel thorn at both entrance and exit and crawled in, leaving only the lone sentry outside in the freezing pre-dawn cold. Five minutes later they were all fast asleep as if they hadn't a worry in the world.

Chapter Two

'*Morgen, meine Herren,*' despite his desert sores and persistent jaundice, Rommel, the Desert Fox, was as brisk as ever as he strode into his headquarters.

'*Morgen, Herr General,*' the assembled staff officers snapped as one, as they clicked to attention.

Rommel waved his fly whisk at them to indicate they should stand at ease, and put his cap and whisk down on the side of the table bearing the big map of the Western Desert. 'I see you have made considerable progress since yesterday,' he commented staring at the rash of chinograph marks which had appeared on it since he had last seen it.

Westphal, his chief-of-staff, said, 'The Tommies are in total confusion. It will be an ideal time to strike.' He crushed his hand against the side of his shaven head, as if he were checking there was no hair there, and added with a stiff smile on his hard face. 'This time we will push them all the way back to Cairo and that will be the end of the English Eighth Army.'

There was a murmur of agreement from the other officers.

'That is exactly what I will tell the macaronis when I fly to Rome this day.' He chuckled suddenly, the tough pugnacious face relaxing for a moment, 'The news will probably make their Duce green with envy. The last time *he* proposed to drive the English back to the Egyptian capital, he even had his white horse sent to Libya so that he could ride in triumph into Cairo. Unfortunately, as we all know, it didn't happen that way. That's why we of the *Afrikakorps* are here.'

'Yes, unfortunately,' Westphal agreed. 'After all it's in Russia where the really decisive battles are taking place, not out here in this backwater, pulling out hot chestnuts from the fire for the macaronis.'

'Yes,' someone else said, 'Why do we have to go to all this trouble to tell the Italians what we are about? We're doing the real fighting not their contemptible army.'

Rommel answered the protest patiently. 'The Führer, in his infinite wisdom, has

195

always made it his policy to pander a little to the sensibilities of these other nations, as long as it suits his purpose. Allies and ex-enemies alike—Italians, French, Rumanians, Croatians and the rest of them—they don't really count. Only we Germans count. We are Europe's leaders.'

'Here, here!' his staff officers agreed stoutly, faces suddenly set and proud.

'The 20th century is German's century, *our* century. But our beloved Führer, Adolf Hitler, still allows these subjects to believe they can make independent decisions. Hence the reason for my damn flight to Rome this day.'

'The journey to Rome has a positive side to it as, well, *Herr General.*' It was Meyer, his Chief of Intelligence.

'How do you mean, Meyer?' Rommel snapped, staring at the thin greying officer with the clever eyes hidden behind gold-rimmed spectacles.

Meyer took his time. It was as if he were weighing every single word before he uttered it. 'All indications are, *Herr General,*' he said thoughtfully and softly so that the other officers had to strain to catch his words, 'that the English are planning...an attempt on your...life.'

'What?' Rommel exploded in amazement.

'Impossible.' Westphal snapped dismissively. 'Such a thing would go totally against the Tommies' sense of fair play. No, that's not possible.'

Meyer stood his ground. 'We have proof,' he said in that pedantic thoughtful manner of his, 'that the English have several teams from these new commandos of theirs intent on the assassination of Herr Rommel.'

Rommel laughed. 'Oh, well, let us not dwell on the matter. By the time they reach us—if they ever do, *Oberst* Meyer—I shall be safely tucked away in Rome, eating all that disgusting muck that the Italians call food. Give me a good old German *Bratwurst und Sauerkraut* any day.'

The others laughed and the matter of the assassination plot was dropped.

Five minutes later Rommel was marching briskly out of the HQ, leather coat swinging in the desert wind, rapping out orders as he strode towards the waiting *Horch*, while staff officers trotted behind him like little dogs, busily scribbling in their notebooks. 'Keep my right flank strong...see the panzer divisions are closer to the main battle line...mass the 88s...in front of the infantry if necessary...' And then the big camouflaged car was rolling towards the main coastal road, with Rommel still bellowing orders through the open window at his exhausted staff...

O'Sullivan lay on the top of the 'hide' surveying the road and the buildings beyond with his binoculars. Next to him Smith 175 did the same. As yet it was too early for much traffic to be on the road, a supply truck or two, a captured jeep packed with Italian soldiers in solar topees looking like something from a 20's film, and a shot-up German tank being taken to the workshops to the rear.

Smith 175 lowered his own glasses and said, 'I'm fair clem, sir. Could do with a mug o'char something awful.'

''Fraid no can do, Smithie. The CO's ordered no brew up until it's dark again. You'll have to make do with water.'

Smith 175 shuddered dramatically. 'Water!' he exclaimed in mock horror, 'where I come from they say water rusts yer guts.'

O'Sullivan started to laugh, but the laugh froze on his lips when he saw the big open staff car coming down the road, the stiff metal flag of a senior officer at its bonnet, gleaming in the rising sun. He focused his glasses swiftly.

'Christ!' he hissed when the face of the man in the backseat entered the gleaming circles of glass.

'What is it, sir?' Smith 175 asked urgently.

O'Sullivan didn't answer. He concentrated on that lone figure in the back of the big staff car, wanting to make absolutely sure he was right. The memory of the wounded Gore-Smythe, with only minutes to go before he was killed, flashed into his mind, 'The Desert Fox...bloody Rommel... The cause of all our troubles!' he had snorted angrily that terrible day when their company had been virtually wiped out. Yes, it was him all right. No mistake. There sat the arch enemy of the Eighth Army.

Moments later he was shaking Stirling awake to tell him the surprising news, while Paddy Mayne, hair tousled, eyes heavy with sleep, listened in disbelief.

'Are you sure?' Stirling asked finally, 'It's vitally important.'

'Yes, I'm sure,' O'Sullivan answered. 'He's the same man I saw that day with poor old Gore-Symthe.'

'Christ, that's torn it, Paddy Mayne snorted. 'What do we do now? There's no way we can warn Keyes that the op is really off. That the target's flown.'

Stirling shook his head. 'No, there isn't.' His mind raced furiously as he tried to work out what to do next. Something had to come out of it for the Special Air Service, he knew that. Otherwise those brass-hats in Cairo would soon close down the SAS's shop. Keyes would have targeted Rommel's HQ, so he might shoot up a few of Rommel's staff officers there. But what could the SAS do that would make the new unit look good?

'All right,' he said quickly, as he rolled out of his blankets and knelt in the still cold sand. 'Here's the generator,' he marked the place in the sand with his forefinger. 'We'll knock that out as planned.'

Paddy Mayne's face lit up when he realized that they were going to see some action after all. 'Good show, David!' he chortled eagerly. 'Carry on.'

'Then we'll booby-trap Rommel's private quarters. With a bit of luck we might just get him when he returns from wherever he's gone to.'

Mayne chuckled. 'Music to my poor old ears, David, he said enthusiastically. 'And what then?'

'This. Bill here,' he nodded to O'Sullivan, 'will take a stick and set up the bren outside the police barracks—here,' he marked the spot in the sand. 'Once the jolly old generator goes up in the sky, I 'spect they'll come tumbling out of their barracks. Bill and his stick will give them all they've got till the fur and snot begins to fly. Then they'll do a hasty bunk and join up with the rest of us.

By then Keyes and his commando laddies will have discovered that the show's not on and will probably be retreating towards us. We'll cover them as best we can while we make for the RV. What do you think?'

Paddy Mayne saw no objections. As there was the prospect of a scrap, he was all for it. 'It's going to be a fine party, David,' he declared.

Stirling looked at O'Sullivan when the latter did not respond. 'Well, Bill, what do you think?'

'Oh, I'll go along with it, sir,' the other officer replied. 'But it seems to me a bit iffy and chancey as well.'

'What do you mean?'

'Well, sir,' O'Sullivan said a little helplessly. 'Not only will we be fighting the Jerries, but we might also be fighting Colonel Keyes' commandos as well. They won't know we're there—'

'Ach,' Paddy Mayne cut him short, 'You're seeing problems where there are none, laddie. It'll all come out in the wash, believe you me, Bill.'

'I suppose you're right, Paddy,' O'Sullivan said reluctantly, but he wasn't really convinced.

'All right, then we move out,' Stirling said, looking at his watch, 'at eighteen hundred hours. Now any questions?'

Chapter Three

Midnight.

Keyes raised his hand, as if giving a signal, and said softly, 'All right, chaps, we're off.'

Obediently the commandos, laden down with weapons and equipment started to move forward, bodies bent against the pelting rain which was already soaking them to the skin. But they were used to hardship and didn't complain, save one slipped on the muddy trail and cursed.

Up at the front of the long file, Keyes alternately checked the inky blackness to his front, his face wet with raindrops, and the green-glowing dial of the prismatic compass strapped to his left wrist.

He had estimated originally that it might take them just over an hour to reach the first escarpment. But now he revised that estimate, due to the darkness and appalling weather conditions.

Time passed. The only sounds were the persistent hiss of the cold rain and the occasional clink of equipment. The weather was absolutely rotten, Keyes told himself, as he staggered and slipped along the trail laden down with fifty pounds of equipment just like the rest, but it did have one advantage. No one who could possibly avoid it would want to be out on a night like this.

At just after one he spotted the dark outline of the first escarpment ahead. From the maps he knew it was some two hundred and fifty feet. It would be tough even for his trained commandos, especially at night and in this rain storm, he knew. But it had to be done and it *would* be done.

At two o'clock that terrible night the rain-soaked men reached the foot of the rock and turf wall, where Keyes rested them for a few minutes while he searched for the track which he knew led up it. He found it and calling the men again, said, 'We'll go up in single file. Keep as quiet as possible. If there's trouble, only use firearms as a last resort. Got it?'

There was a murmur of assent from the men. They didn't need to be warned. They all knew that they were entering the danger zone now. The German barracks with their hundreds of soldiers and military policemen were only a couple of miles away.

Keyes took a deep breath. Then he placed his right foot on the steep muddy trail and began the ascent. It was tough going. Men slipped and fell. Others cursed and yelped with pain as they grabbed the camel thorn on both sides of the trail for support. And all the while the cold rain beat down relentlessly.

They were half way up, panting and lathered with sweat in spite of the cold, when a dog started barking, harsh and hysterical. They froze, hardly daring to breathe. Slowly, very slowly, Keyes started to unsling his tommy gun with its silencer. If the worse came to the worse, he'd shoot the beast dead before it alarmed the whole neighbourhood.

Suddenly a yellow knife of light came from a hut which he had not spotted up to now. A voice shouted at the dog. It continued to bark. There was the sound of boots squelching through the mud. Keyes tensed. It was now or never. Still the barking continued. There was a soft thud. The dog's barking turned into a yelp of pain. The boots squelched back through the mud. The yellow light vanished. All was silence once more.

'Just then I could have pissed mesen,' one of the commandos behind Keyes whispered hoarsely.

'What d'yer mean—*could*,' his mate whispered back. 'I *did*.'

Keyes laughed shakily.

They moved on again.

204

They had almost reached the top of the steep escarpment when Keyes spotted the machine gun nest, or that was what he thought it had to be. At first he couldn't make out what the little red light was piercing the inky darkness, then he heard a soft cough and realized immediately, it was a sentry smoking a cigarette. Behind him now Keyes could see the sandbags of what he took was a machine gun guarding the exit to the trail.

He turned on the stalled column. 'Sergeant,' he whispered softly to the man behind him. 'Detail four men. Drop your packs and equipment. There are Jerries over there at eleven o'clock. Got 'em?'

'Got 'em, sir.'

'Nobble 'em, then.'

He caught the white gleam of the sergeant's teeth in the rain-soaked gloom, as he whispered, 'With the greatest of pleasure, sir.'

Keyes nodded his approval. His men were trained professionals.

They needed no further orders.

Hastily, but noiselessly, the NCO and the four commandos slipped out of their heavy packs and lowered them to the ground. They propped their weapons against the packs and then they were off, heading for the rear of the little bunker. Keyes flashed a look at his watch. He estimated it would take them five minutes to get into position. He prayed that the lone sentry wouldn't turn and spot the dark figures stealing up on his post.

In his head he counted off the seconds. Suddenly, startlingly, there was a swiftly muffled groan. The little red light vanished. He cocked his head to one side and strained. He heard a sound. It was like something hard striking a body. Another muffled groan. Moments later the five men came hurrying back, not bothered about making a noise now.

As they came closer, Keyes could see the sergeant was now sporting a pistol in his belt. 'Got mesen a little souvenir,' the NCO gasped and grinned. 'We left a couple of our souvenirs behind...three of 'em, all very dead.'

Moments later they were on their way again. Now Rommel's HQ was only one mile away...

Swiftly and silently, Smith 175 and Dawson set up the bren gun, while the other two covered them and O'Sullivan strained his eyes as he stared at the dark outline of the police barracks.

'OK, sir,' Smith 175 whispered and, pulling back the bolt of the light machine gun, cocked the bren. Next to him Dawson flopped to the ground and started filling up the curved magazines next to the tripod, ready for firing.

'Good,' O'Sullivan answered, feeling the adrenalin beginning to flood through his body at the prospect of action very soon. He turned to the other two. 'You and you, Flood and Hawkins, follow that line of poles till you're a bit away from the barracks and then cut the cables. We'll keep you covered from here.'

'Righto, sir,' the two replied as one and doubled away along the little road by which the cable ran, supported by rough poles.

'Won't be long now, sir,' Smith 175 said in a gentle conversational manner, as if he were talking about the next issue of NAAFI cigarettes. 'I allus thought they said the condemned man ate a hearty breakfast. My guts is doing flip-flops through lack of grub.'

'All right, Smithie,' Dawson, his running mate, hissed, 'put a frigging sock in it. Condemned man indeed.'

O'Sullivan smiled softly. They were good men; he knew he could rely upon them implicitly. His smile vanished. Someone was moving in the darkness to their front and for a moment he caught the beam of a torch shining silver

207

in the pouring rain. *'Freeze,'* he hissed urgently.

'Ich dachte ich hörte was, Fritz,' a voice said.

'Du hast eine bluhende Fantasie, mein Freund,' another voice growled sulkily. *'Komm rein aus dem Scheissregen.'*

There was the sucking, squelching sound once more, as the two men returned to wherever they were quartered for the night. Silence reigned again. After a few moments, Smith 175 said, 'You know, sir, I think we're gonna be lucky on this one after all.'

'Why do you say that?' O'Sullivan asked without too much interest, feeling the raindrops trickle unpleasantly down the small of his back.

'Well, sir, I thought too many chances was being taken. All a bit of a Fred Karno's army like. I told you that, didn't I, Dawson?'

'Yes,' Dawson began, but before he could confirm the rest of Smith's thought, there was a rain-muted bang to their right and for a moment the inky blackness was split by a knife of scarlet flame. An instant later the two others came stumbling and sliding back through the mud to inform them, 'The generator's just been blown and we've cut the wires.'

'Good work,' O'Sullivan snapped hastily

as over at the barracks, lights were being snapped on everywhere despite the blackout and angry, alarmed voices were crying out orders and questions.

'Now the fun and games are going to start,' Dawson commented, as Smith tucked the butt of the bren tighter into his big muscular shoulder.

Dawson was right. Suddenly a flare shot up into the rain-drenched sky, colouring the area all around in its eerie blood-red hue, the raindrops lashing through the glare in silver stitches. There was a roar of a truck being started up.

'Here they come,' O'Sullivan cried urgently and raised his Tommy gun.

The barracks' gate swung open. A big truck started to edge its way out, windscreen wipers jerking back and forth, the white blur of the driver's face visible behind the streaming glass. 'Get him,' O'Sullivan yelled and prepared to fire.

Smith 175 needed no urging. 'Try this one for frigging size!' he cried and pressed the bren's trigger. Tracer sped towards the truck in a lethal morse. There was the crunch of shattered glass, then the driver screamed shrilly. The truck went out of control and slewed right round to slam into the wall of the barracks. Next moment its motor erupted in a burst of angry flame. An instant later the whole truck was burning furiously. No one got out.

'*Alarm...alarm,*' an angry voice yelled furiously. Someone shrilled a whistle. Muted though distinct, even in the heavy beat of the rainstorm, they could hear the sound of running feet.

'Over there, sir,' one of the SAS troopers shouted, 'One o'clock, they're trying to get over the wall.'

O'Sullivan reacted instinctively, pressing the trigger of the tommy gun. The noise was tremendous as the bullets zipped towards the dark figures crawling over the wall.

Screams, yells for help, curses. A dozen men went reeling backwards in the same moment that one of the grenades they were carrying exploded outlining their dying shocked faces a dramatic lurid red.

A grenade came sailing their way.

'Duck...hit the dirt!' O'Sullivan yelled.

They did as it exploded five yards away sending cruel slivers of razor sharp metal flying everywhere. And then from all around guns were firing, explosive charges were being detonated and with a banshee-like howl mortar bombs were rising into the sky, flares shouting aloft—the whole terrible irrational music of war. The battle for Rommel's HQ had commenced in earnest.

Chapter Four

Keyes clattered up the steps of the villa. His Tommy gun was cocked and ready. Behind him two of his commandos did the same. All three of them were tense and expectant. From all sides there came bangs and explosions. It was evident that the Germans were now on the alert.

'Hit the doors,' Keyes began.

Too late!

The glass door was swung open. A German in a steel helmet stood there, looking at them in the slice of yellow light that escaped from the Rommel villa as if in bewilderment.

Suddenly he opened his mouth as if to shout a warning. Keyes rammed his Tommy gun at him. The German reacted unexpectedly. He grabbed hold of the weapon and pulled the young Colonel towards him. Together they fell against a wall. Desperately a frantic Keyes reached for his knife. He couldn't get it. Behind him one of the commandos pulled the trigger of his revolver. The .32 spat fire. The German shrieked with unbearable pain. His face shattered, his features fell to his chest like molten red sealing wax. He let go of Keyes' Tommy gun.

'Come on, chaps!' Keyes shouted, knowing now that the other Germans in the villa must have heard the shot. 'Let's get his nibs.'

'With you, sir!' the others yelled.

'Use your weapons at will. They've heard us all right,' Keyes cried and they rushed forward through the glass doors into a large stone hall. The place was dimly lit and it was hard to see. But they heard the clatter of heavy nailed boots all right. There was somebody about.

A door opened. Someone was clattering down the stairs. One of the commandos fired a burst before the German came into sight. He turned and fled the way that he had come. 'Sod that for a lark,' the commando who had fired yelled, and raced up the stairs.

Meanwhile Keyes had begun opening the doors that led off the hall. The first one was empty. From the second there came some light. He flung the door open. A group of helmeted Germans filled the place. Some were still sitting. Others were already on their feet, alerted, weapons in their hands. Keyes slammed the door shut. 'I'm going to throw a grenade in,' he yelled to the commandos behind him. 'Here goes.'

'Don't forget the diver,' one of them chanted, a fair imitation of the funny character in the ITMA radio show.

Keyes didn't smile. He was too tense.

They tensed.

Keyes pulled the pin from the Mills bomb. Hurriedly he counted off the seconds, the grenade red-hot in his right hand. 'Right.' He flung open the door. The grenade sailed into the middle of the room. The Germans' eyes widened with horror as they stared fixedly at the little metal egg which had landed so surprisingly in their midst.

'Good show,' Keyes began and reached for the door knob. One of the Germans reacted more quickly. He fired. Keyes yelled with pain. His hand clutched at his chest above the heart. Next moment he slammed to the ground unconscious.

One of the commandos pulled the body to one side. Another grabbed the knob and slammed the door shut. There was a muffled thump. Thick black smoke poured from beneath the door. Silence followed the explosion. The light had gone out. The commandos reasoned they had killed or knocked out the Germans inside.

'Let's get the colonel out of the firing line,' one of them gasped. 'He looks as if he's in a bad way, mate.'

Together a handful of them dragged

Keyes away from the door. Then they lifted him and carried him outside, while the villa erupted with further small arms firing, the flashes of the weapons stabbing the darkness. A sergeant undid Keyes' battledress blouse hurriedly. He bent and listened intently. He lifted his head and crouched there grimly in silence.

'How bad is he Sarge?' one of the commandos asked.

'He's dead,' the sergeant answered, voice full of emotion. 'The Colonel's dead.'

A moment later they were running for their lives, steaming into the desert, as behind them the Germans, blind with rage and frustration, fired shot after shot at them. The Rommel mission had failed...

'A tank, sir,' Dawson yelled urgently.

'Frig that for a lark,' one of the SAS troopers cried and started to clamber from his hole, as if he were going to make a run for it.

'Get down,' O'Sullivan ordered angrily. 'We'll stop the bugger. Smithie, aim at the Jerry in the turret. He deserves to go for a Burton, standing up like that. Silly fart in a trance.'

Smith 175 flung up the bren. In one and the same movement, he aimed and fired. At that range he couldn't miss... With a shrill hysterical scream the tank

214

commander threw up his hands as if in despair before flopping over the edge of the turret, either dead or dying.

The sudden burst unnerved the tank driver in his compartment below. He tugged at the brake levers. The tank slithered round in a cloud of sudden dust. Next instant the nose of the Mark III smashed into the side of the gate and blocked it completely.

'Good show,' O'Sullivan yelled exuberantly. 'But keep on firing, chaps. We've got 'em all nicely bottled up for the time being.'

New heart returned to the little band of hard-pressed SAS men.

The troopers started firing short sharp bursts to left and right, the whole length of the barracks' wall. Men trying to scale it, fell back, shrieking and clutching ruined faces or simply sprawled there in silence. Here and there, there were cries for stretcher-bearers. One poor wretch, blinded by a British bullet, kept calling, *'Sanitater...Sani...ich bin blind. Gott helfe mir...'* But on this terrible night, God must have been looking the other way and no stretcher-bearer rushed to help. In the end O'Sullivan put a bullet into the blinded man to finish him off for good.

But even above the angry snap-and-crackle of the small arms battle, O'Sullivan

215

could hear the rusty rattle of tank tracks. The Germans were bringing up another tank to clear the exit to the barracks. O'Sullivan heard the hollow boom as metal struck metal. The jammed Mark III tank squeaked and groaned in protest as the unseen tank behind it began to push.

'All right, chaps,' O'Sullivan cried above the racket, knowing that as soon as the exit was clear all hell would be let loose, 'let's make a run for it—*now!*'

They needed no urging. All of them knew that time was running out for them—fast. Smith 175 picked up the steaming bren gun, its barrel a glowing dull pink, as if it were a child's toy. The troopers grabbed their weapons and started to back off, while O'Sullivan covered their retreat. Standing there, legs spread like a western gunslinger in some cowboy movie, he fired controlled bursts to left and right, trying desperately to keep the Germans behind the wall, while at the gate the Mark III tank was slowly but surely pushed to one side.

'Die Tommies haben ab!' someone cried angrily in German.

O'Sullivan, panting as if he were running a great race, guessed the enemy had tumbled to the fact that they were retreating. He started to move back, too, firing all the while.

But now the Germans had recovered

from their surprise. More and more of them were attempting to clamber over the wall. Others poised there, firing wildly into the darkness. One final shove and the crippled tank was pushed clear. The second cmcrgcd from the gate to the barracks, its turret machine gun already spitting angry scarlet fire.

O'Sullivan broke off his covering action. Slinging his Tommy gun, he ran after the rest, disappearing into the glowing darkness, bullets zipping lethally through the air all around him.

Behind the fugitives the barracks seemed to have gone crazy. Signal flares shot into the air on all sides. Machine guns chattered. Whistles were shrilled. Orders— and counter orders—were barked urgently. It was total chaotic confusion and, as he pelted into the desert, O'Sullivan told himself that it was all in their favour. The Germans obviously didn't know as yet what was going on. They were firing in a dozen different directions. It was the kind of cock-up they needed to effect their escape. For O'Sullivan knew instinctively that something had gone badly wrong with the plan to kill Rommel. Now it was every man for himself, and he was determined to bring his own little group through, come what may. His first duty now was to his troopers.

'Keep on going,' he gasped as he caught up with the last of the little group, to a trooper who seemed to be faltering. 'In a couple of minutes we'll be safe and out of this shit—' He stopped short. A couple of blacked out headlights had appeared on the coastal road to their left.

Smith in the lead stopped instinctively. He called, 'Lorry coming up.'

'Down!' O'Sullivan commanded.

They dropped as one. They peered through the darkness. In the flash of an explosion, they caught a fleeting glimpse of the driver, as he hunched over the wheel, driving the vehicle at a snail's pace.

'Eyetie,' Smith 175 whispered to O'Sullivan, as he recognized the uniform.

'Do you think you could get him?'

'Easy as falling off a log,' Smith 175 answered scornfully.

'Then do so.'

'Ain't gonna do his windscreen much good, sir.'

'No matter. Just stop him, we need those wheels, Smithie.'

Smith 175 threw up the bren gun and fired. The red tracer bullets flew towards the slow-moving truck like a flight of angry hornets. There was the sound of splintering glass. A scream. The truck lurched, rolled on a few more paces and then came to an awkward halt.

'Good for you, Smithie,' O'Sullivan said exuberantly. 'You've done it. Come on!'

Behind them they could hear the Germans getting closer. They'd picked up the scent. Urgently they doubled across to the stationary truck. The driver lay sprawled across the wheel, his jet-black greasy hair sprinkled with broken glass. Dawson caught hold of him by the collar and heaved him up. His head lolled to one side. 'Dead,' he said, 'Poor sod, even if he was an Eyetie. Can't be a day older than eighteen.'

O'Sullivan who was only nineteen himself made no comment. Instead he ordered, 'Get him out—gildly. The Jerries are onto us.'

Unceremoniously they hauled the dead Italian driver out and dropped him at the side of the vehicle. With the butt of his Tommy gun, Dawson knocked out the rest of the glass, while another SAS trooper slid behind the wheel, which was sticky with the Italian's blood.

Now they could hear the approaching German tank quite clearly, and the cries of the infantry who were coming up with it. 'Start up,' O'Sullivan yelled.

The trooper turned the key. There was a dull groan, but the engine didn't start.

'For ferking Chrissake,' Smith 175

yelled angrily. 'Get yer frigging finger out, mucker.'

Desperately the trooper at the wheel tried again.

From their right came a tremendous crack. Scarlet flame stabbed the darkness. There was a great howling sound like a giant piece of canvas being ripped apart forcibly. Ten yards away sand and pebbles flew into the air as the tank's shell exploded. Pebbles rained down onto the cab as the engine spluttered into noisy life. The others cheered. Next moment the harassed trooper had thrust home first gear and they were bumping away into the night, the sound of the firing dying away behind them rapidly. They had their wheels.

Chapter Five

'What a balls-up!' Paddy Mayne exploded.

It was dawn. Behind them tracer zigzagged lethally through the ugly-white sky. Fires raged everywhere, with great columns of thick black smoke ascending to the heavens.

'How?' Stirling said throatily, as he paused next to the Irish giant.

'Well, use your eyes, David,' Paddy said

gruffly. 'We've lost half of our effectives, either dead or missing.' He pointed to the two jeeps packed with the seriously wounded, 'And there's not much we can do for those poor sods until we reach our own lines—*if* we do.'

Stirling pulled a face for a moment, then he brightened up again in that enthusiastic manner of his. 'I know, Paddy, I know. We've taken a bad beating. But on the whole, I think the op, has been a success, don't you? Even if Keyes gets the kudos of having bumped off Rommel, we've certainly put the SAS on the map this time.' He beamed at the bigger man.

Paddy Mayne didn't reply. But a hard little voice at the back of his mind rasped, bugger the SAS. Putting the SAS on the map has cost too many good lives. Aloud he said, 'I wonder how young O'Sullivan is getting on?'

'Oh, he'll be all right,' Stirling said confidently, 'That young feller is made of the right stuff. He'll muddle through all right all by himself.'

'I hope so—' Paddy Mayne stopped short. He cocked his head to one side, the weary look vanished from his craggy face to be replaced by one of tension.

'What is it, Paddy?'

'A plane, coming this way,' Mayne snapped back.

'Christ, I see it,' Stirling gasped.

About three hundred yards away, a light plane was almost hovering, as it dropped a flare to illuminate the desert floor below.

'Stop the jeeps!' Stirling bellowed.

The two drivers braked hard and the wounded groaned with the pain of the sudden halt, as the troopers on foot dropped to the sand, hiding their faces as they did so. 'For what we're about to receive, may the Good Lord make us truly thankful,' someone mocked in a funeral tone.

'Shut up!' Stirling snapped urgently.

The light reconnaissance plane started to come closer, as they waited there, hardly daring to breathe. Suddenly, startlingly, Paddy Mayne, his eyes blazing furiously, sprang to his feet.

'Paddy,' Stirling called in alarm. 'What the hell are you up to, man?'

'Fuck this for a game o'soldiers,' Paddy snarled. He sprang to the nearest jeep. One big hand grasped the bren and wrenched it from its tripod in the same instant that he was bathed in the brilliant, icy-white light of another flare.

Handling the heavy machine gun effortlessly, as if it were a child's toy, Paddy Mayne aimed, ignoring the slugs striking up vicious spurts of blue all around him. He was consumed by a burning rage.

Wouldn't the bloody Jerries ever leave 'em in peace? They'd had enough, bloody well more than enough. He pressed the trigger.

The tracer zipped in a white stream upward. It caught the German pilot by surprise. He must have thought he had everything under control. Now he learned that he hadn't. The little plane's engine coughed, spluttered, stopped, started up once more and then went dead completely.

Trooper Hyde, lying in a pool of his own blood, leg severed at the knee, cheered weakly. 'It's the frigging luck o' the Irish,' he said in an Ulster accent, 'You've got the frigger, sir.'

Paddy Mayne had. For a moment he caught a glimpse of the pilot, face beneath the goggles frantic with fear, fighting the controls. Next instant the light plane was screeching out of the sky, totally out of control, plunging to its doom. One moment later it hit the desert floor and exploded in a great red roaring ball of fire.

Stirling frowned. 'That's very bad form, Paddy,' he said severely.

Paddy Mayne tossed the bren back into the jeep carelessly. 'Just another frigging Jerry we don't have to worry about,' he said.

'Yes, we won't have to. But his bloody

223

superiors will. They'll be out looking for him soon enough. As if we didn't have troubles enough, man.'

'Ah, put a sock in it, Stirling,' Mayne said angrily, clenching that big jaw of his. Stirling remembered how Paddy had struck his CO, Keyes, and chased him out of the mess with a bayonet. He decided it would be unwise to say anything else to the big Ulsterman. So, he said instead, 'All right chaps, on your feet. Let's make tracks while we've still got chance.'

Wearily the exhausted SAS troopers clambered to their feet. The jeep drivers started their engines. The wounded groaned anew. The miserable trek ever westwards commenced once more...

Two miles or more away, O'Sullivan saw the sudden burst of flame outlined against the stark dawn sky and guessed what had happened. Another group of the assault force had just shot down an enemy plane which had obviously been searching for them—he had heard it buzzing around the dawn sky for the last fifteen minutes. He breathed out hard. There'd be another up soon looking for them, and the enemy ground forces would be on their way, as soon as they were informed about the place where the plane had been shot down.

O'Sullivan shot an anxious look through the truck's shattered windscreen to where

Dawson poised ready to start the vehicle up once more. The starter motor had gone. Now the big Guardsman would have to turn the engine with the help of the starting handle.

Dawson spat on his big paws and then he inserted the handle. 'Get a frigging move on,' his old running mate, Smith 175, encouraged him. 'There's something moving over there!'

O'Sullivan flung a glance in the direction Smith was indicating.

A cloud of dust flung up by some fast-moving vehicle was coming in there, heading straight for the stalled truck.

'I'm doing my bloody best,' Dawson grunted as he took the strain.

'Then do bloody *better*,' Smith 175 retorted, 'or they'll catch us up the frigging creek without a frigging paddle.'

O'Sullivan focused his glass. A big halftrack, crowded with helmeted troops, slid into the gleaming circles of calibrated glass. He groaned. It was a German all right.

Dawson swung the big handle, knowing that if he got it wrong, the starting handle would swing back at a rapid rate and probably break both his wrists. Despite the dawn cold, the beads of sweat ran down his unshaven face like opaque pearls. Nothing happened.

Now, faintly, he could hear the cries in German. They had been spotted. Desperately he tried again, his shoulder muscles bulging through the thin material of his khaki shirt. Up on the roof of the truck, the bren gunner lying full length had begun to fire. Like glowing golf balls, the Germans returned the fire with a small cannon mounted next to the driver's cab. Sand began to erupt in violent spurts all around the stranded truck.

There was a groan, a doleful spluttering, a kind of mechanical keening. Frantically Dawson prayed the engine would start now. If it didn't—he couldn't think that particular miserable thought to its logical end. Suddenly, almost startlingly, the engine fired. Behind the wheel, the trooper driving gunned the engine madly. The morning air was abruptly full of the cloying stink of petrol. 'Come on,' Smith 175 yelled above the boom of the German cannon, 'move your arse! Get in!'

Dawson dropped the starting handle, as if it was red-hot. He started to run to the back of the truck. In that same instant a shell exploded some twenty yards or so away. Shrapnel scythed through the air with lethal ferocity. Dawson yelled. His hands flailed in the air wildly, as if he were climbing the rungs of an invisible ladder.

'Christ,' Smith 175 cried, 'what yer gone and done, yer silly bugger!'

Dawson went down on his knees. Smith and another trooper dropped to the ground. Hastily they gathered up the wounded man, the bright red blood arcing from a great gap in his back. 'I'm all right,' Dawson began and fainted. Smith 175 and the other man shoved him full-length into the back of the vehicle. Another shell exploded nearby. The truck rocked alarmingly. Next to a panting Smith 175, the trooper who had helped him fell flat on his face. He was dead before he hit the floor of the truck.

'Get going, driver!' O'Sullivan bellowed above the boom of the German gun, as the halftrack, trailing a wake of flying sand behind it, came ever closer.

The trooper slammed home first gear. Next moment they were bouncing and jolting across the desert, leaving a trail of blood—and petrol—behind them...

Chapter Six

'I think I'm dying sir,' Dawson croaked, as they crouched in the bit of shade from the midday sun which the patch of camel thorn offered.

It was an hour now since the last of the petrol had drained from the punctured tank of the lorry and they had been forced to abandon it.

For a while Dawson had managed to stagger along with the other three survivors, then his legs had given way beneath him like those of a newly born calf and Smith 175 had gathered him up in his big arms and carried him. Now Dawson could go on no longer and Smith 175 was too exhausted to carry him any more. So they rested, tongues hanging out like those of overheated, parched dogs, and wondered how they were to carry on any more.

'Course you're not you silly twat,' Smith 175 objected, his voice seeming to come from a long, long way off. 'You'll live to be a hund—' Dawson's eyes had turned upwards so that only the white could be seen. The end of his nose had become strangely white and pinched too. Smith 175 knew the signs. He had seen them often enough before. They were those of a man about to die, 'Hey, come off it,' he demanded angrily and grabbed the front of Dawson's blood-soaked shirt as if he were about to shake him.

Dawson's eyes flickered open weakly. Slowly, very slowly, they came into focus and spotted Smith 175 looking down on him. 'Yer can have my shaving mirror, the metal one. You were allus after it, yer crafty sod, Smithie.' He tried to smile, but failed miserably.

'Now none of that talk here,' Smith barked, his voice gaining in strength, as if he were angry with the dying man. 'Don't go on frigging well saying things like that—daft, I call it.'

'Ta, ta, Smithie. Remember the mirr—' Dawson's voice faded into nothing. Slowly his head lolled to one side.

Hastily Smith pulled the metal shaving mirror out of Dawson's left breast pocket, rubbed it on his sleeve and held the mirror close to his old pal's mouth. No breath disturbed its polished surface. 'Fuck it,' he said slowly, almost reflectively, 'he's gone and snuffed it.'

Wearily O'Sullivan turned his head, as if it were worked by rusty springs and stared down at Dawson, with his mouth gaping open stupidly. 'Yes, he's dead, Smithie.'

Smith 175 looked around in some bewilderment. 'How are we gonna bury him?' he asked of no one in particular. 'We ain't even got a shovel.'

'We'll just leave him,' O'Sullivan answered gently. He knew the two ex-Guardsmen had been together ever since long before the war. 'The Jerries'll find

229

him in the end. They'll bury him. They're good at that, you know.'

'But he'll just be an unknown soldier, sir,' Smith 175 objected. 'I'm not having that...' He struggled to his feet, reaching for the jackknife dangling from his webbing belt.

Ten minutes later he had fashioned a crude cross of camel thorn wood, carved with the words, 'Trooper R. Dawson, 1085056. B. 1915, K.I.A. 1941. 1st SAS.' Grimly Smith 175 planted it next to the dead body, took one of Dawson's identity discs and his paybook. Then as an afterthought he placed the purple beret with its flaming sword badge gently over the dead face. Quietly he read out the words once more and then, as if speaking to himself, he said, 'Not bloody much to show for a lifetime.'

Five minutes later they were on their way again, heading westwards. Behind them the desert wind already began to waft sand over the dead body...

'Mekili,' O'Sullivan announced, as they went to ground and stared at the large white painted fort to their front, surrounded by Arab shacks and ramshackle buildings. 'The Eyeties probably still hold it. But I'm not worried particularly about that. If we can hide out till nightfall, I

230

think we'll be able to rustle up some grub and water from inside the fort without too much trouble. The Eyeties are not the best of sentries, are they?'

Smith 175 said nothing. Obviously he was still upset by the death of his old comrade. But the other trooper said hoarsely, 'A bit of grub would go down right nice, sir. Even bully beef and dog biscuits.' He licked his parched cracked lips, as if in anticipation.

'You see that low building to the right of the fort?' O'Sullivan continued. 'If I'm right that's the place where the Arabs put their dead. In this dry heat the corpses are preserved for years, but the Arabs never go near such places unless it's to place their dead there. I think that would be a good place to lie low till nightfall.'

'Cor stone the crows,' the trooper said a little apprehensively. 'That's a right turn up for the books, sir.'

'All right,' O'Sullivan said, rising wearily, 'let's get on with it. And watch how we go.'

It was raining again. As a result the Arabs were sticking close to their miserable little huts. They could hear them and could smell camel dung and the pungent spices with which they made their half-rotten food palatable, but they couldn't see them.

Now with O'Sullivan in the lead, they pushed their way into the house of death, noting as they did so that no one had been here for a long time: the dust was thick on the floor and there were no footprints in it. O'Sullivan nodded his approval. That was all to the good. If no one died in the Arab village this day, they would be safe enough here.

He pressed on, turned a bend in the gloomy corridor and stopped abruptly with a shocked gasp.

'What is it, sir?' Smith 175 whispered, keeping his voice low, as if he were awed by their surroundings in this house of death.

'Over there,' O'Sullivan answered, also in a whisper.

Smith 175 peered over the young officer's shoulder and gasped, too. 'Christ Almighty,' he said in an awed voice, 'it's a frigging mummy, sir.'

'Something like that,' O'Sullivan agreed, staring at the skeletal figure propped against the wall of the corridor. It was a dull leather colour, clad in rags and shrouded with dusty cobwebs. But it was the skeletal face which shocked them. For the lips were formed into a cracked and dreadful sort of smile under eye sockets which were black and empty.

The trooper crossed himself hastily, and said, 'Holy Mary, Mother of God, help and protect.' Then he added, 'Sir, there's dozens o'em, all down the corridor.'

There were. Men, women and even children stretching right into shadows. To O'Sullivan they looked like some ghastly queue, waiting to go—he didn't quite know where. He pulled himself together. 'All right,' he said, iron in his voice, 'take no notice of them. They're dead. They can't do us any harm. The living Eyeties can. Now we're going to get some shuteye before it gets dark. Smithie, you take first stag. Wake me in an hour, then I'll stand my spell. All right, Trooper, get yer head down for a two hour kip.'

Keeping his eyes on the line of dead bodies propped against the opposite wall, the young soldier did as ordered. But it seemed an age, so Smith 175 standing guard thought, before their snores indicated that the two men had finally gone to sleep.

Grimly Smith 175 sat cross-legged in the middle of the corridor, O'Sullivan's Colt in his big hand, staring at the dead woman propped against the wall opposite him. Once she might have been pretty, for he judged her to have died young. Now through the open robe, he could see that her breasts were shrivelled and empty so that they looked like dry leather pouches. He shivered a little and wondered if this was what would happen to poor old Dawsie. Would he lie out there in the desert till the flesh fell from his bones and his skin became as tanned as leather by the desert sun? He shook his head at the thought and dismissed it. It didn't do any good, he told himself, thinking that way in this house of death.

He forced himself to think of the future. He guessed that it might take them another forty-eight hours to reach the Eighth Army's lines. If they could get some grub inside themselves this night, they'd make it, he knew. Both the young officer and Trooper Hare were in fair nick. All they needed was something to eat.

Time passed leadenly. More than once Smith 175 found himself nodding off and was jerked awake with a start. From outside the muted noise from the Arab hamlet grew even less. He reasoned it was slowly getting dark. He looked at the green glowing dial of his wrist-watch. His hour was well up, but he didn't have the heart to wake up O'Sullivan. He was an old sweat—he was used to long hours on guard duty. He didn't need as much kip as the two younger men.

More time passed. Now it was quite dark in the house of death and Smith 175 found that his eyes were beginning to play tricks with him in the gloomy corridor. Several times he could have sworn that the dead bodies propped against the wall had moved. He was one hundred per cent sure that the ragged fabric of the dead woman's robe had moved too. 'Christ, Smithie,' he cursed unwardly at himself, 'get a frigging grip of yersen. You'll be going doolally next, mate.'

The woman's tattered rags moved again. This time Smith 175 knew he was not imagining things, for at the same time that the woman's robe fluttered, he could feel a breath of cooler air coming into that fetid house of death. Someone had opened the door!

Smith 175 acted swiftly. He bent and pressed his hand over O'Sullivan's mouth, while at the same time he whispered urgently into the officer's ear. 'Somebody on the prowl.'

O'Sullivan woke immediately, as Smith did the same to Hare.

For a few moments, their hearts beating frantically, they waited in the gloom, weapons at the ready.

Suddenly, startlingly, a great black shadow was cast on the wall behind them. Smith 175 stifled a gasp of surprise.

'Somebody with a torch,' O'Sullivan whispered. 'Reflection.'

At his side, Hare whispered, 'Thank Christ for that. Scared the breeches off'n me, it did.'

A moment later a small man, torch in hand, came round the bend and stopped dead, his fact suddenly ashen with fear, as he spotted the three men crouched there. *'Porco Madonna!'* he exclaimed, dropping the torch with fright. *'No asbaliato...vado via subito.'* The little man in the shabby grey-green uniform of the Italian Army turned and prepared to make a run for it.

O'Sullivan was quicker off the mark. He dived forward. His right shoulder slammed into the back of the Italian. He went down as if pole-axed, with O'Sullivan sprawled on top of him, frantically fighting to get a hold of the little pistol, which the soldier wore at his right hip. A moment later he had it. He turned and looked up at Smith who had retrieved the Italian's dropped torch. He grinned and pointed to the Italian at his feet, 'I think we've got the key to the quartermaster's stores, Smithie.'

Smith 175, smiling for the first time since Dawson's death, answered. 'I think we have, sir. Lovely grub... Well, lead on MacDuff...'

Chapter Seven

Smith 175 looked expectantly at O'Sullivan, while their Italian prisoner stood there puzzled, wondering probably what was going to happen to him now that the English had stolen the food they needed from the fort and had got outside again without being detected.

O'Sullivan nodded. Smith raised the clubbed pistol and brought it down on the back of the unsuspecting Italian's skull, saying, 'I'm not gonna say this hurts me more than it does you, mate, but I hope it ain't too hard.'

The Italian groaned softly and sank to the sand, out like a light. Smith caught him just in time and lowered him the rest of the way gently.

'Poor little Eyetie sod,' Hare said, mouth full of greasy Italian salami. 'Got us in and out all right, toot sweet.'

'Yes, but let's not stand around here, gossiping like old women,' O'Sullivan snapped, feeling new strength surging through his emaciated body now that he had had a few bites of food. 'The moon's starting to rise.' He indicated the sickle moon which had now appeared from behind the clouds and was beginning to illuminate everything in its stark silver light, 'We don't want any of those sentries up there on the wall spotting us. Let's go.'

They needed no urging. Leaving the unconscious Italian, who so it appeared, had entered the house of the dead to see if there was anything to rob there, in particular the gold teeth which the Arabs favoured, lying on the cold sand, they set off again.

O'Sullivan planned to march till first light—'fifty-five minutes on the hour,' as he had explained to the others, 'then five minutes rest.' Then they'd lie up for the day. As soon as night fell they would set off once more.

'As I see it,' he had lectured them, 'with a bit of luck we'll make it by dawn on the second day. We've got grub and water.' He had grinned at Smith 175, his teeth shining brilliant white against his deeply tanned face, 'And in your case, Smithie, a bottle of chianti as well.'

A happy Smith had replied, 'Sir, man does not live by bread alone. He needs a touch of the old hard stuff as well.'

Five minutes later they were on their way again, happily chewing on salami and excellent Italian white bread, heading ever westwards, all three of the survivors glad that every step they took was yet another on the way to safety...

The harassed infantry commander handed Paddy Mayne and Stirling a mug of whisky and water, with ' 'Fraid there's no ice or soda.'

Paddy Mayne grabbed his and before he drained the liquid from the battered enamel mug, he gasped, 'No matter. The whisky alone will bring roses to my faded cheeks.'

The infantry commander laughed a little wearily. All day long, the Germans had been probing his forward positions and he had lost twenty men that afternoon alone. He guessed he couldn't hold much longer, unless he received reinforcements and fresh supplies. And this handful of battered rags who had wandered into his positions, some thirty minutes before, won't be much help, he reasoned. They had too many wounded of their own and they were exhausted; he could see that.

Outside the dugout another salvo of German shells exploded. The company commander started nervously and Paddy Mayne could see his nerve was virtually gone, so he asked his questions quickly. The sooner they got out of this dangerous place, he told himself, the better. 'Have you heard anything else of our mission, Major?'

The company commander refilled his pipe with a hand that shook badly. 'A bit,' he replied. 'Colonel Keyes is dead. Some of his commandos came through last night. They report he had been shot in the attack on Rommel's HQ.'

'And Rommel?' Stirling queried.

'By all accounts they didn't get him.'

'Bugger!' Stirling retorted and took a fierce sip of his whisky. In reality he wasn't too disappointed. With Keyes dead and Rommel apparently still alive, his own Special Air Service would get better publicity now, he was sure of that.

'And our chaps?' Mayne asked. 'Have any of our chaps passed this way. A chap called O'Sullivan, for instance?'

The company commander shook his head. 'No, you're the only ones from—er— the SAS,' he pronounced the initials as if they were strange to him and he would find it difficult to remember them, 'who have passed this way. O'Sullivan, did you say?' He bit the tip of his old pipe hard, as another batch of 88mm shells exploded outside, making the earth tremble beneath their feet like a live thing. 'No, he's not gone through this sector of the battalion frontier and I would probably have heard from Battalion HQ if he had. No,' he

240

repeated himself, 'you're the only ones.'

Mayne looked at Stirling a little miserably, 'That means we've lost over half our effectives, David,' he said in a soft voice for him. 'Bloody hell!'

Stirling, however, was as buoyant as ever. 'I'm sure we'll be flooded with volunteers once we get back to Cairo and report back what we've done. The very best of the Army will be queuing for a chance to serve with us, believe you me, Paddy.' He shrugged a little carelessly, or so Paddy Mayne thought, 'And don't give up on young Bill O'Sullivan yet. He's made of the right sort of stuff.'

Paddy Mayne grunted but made no comment.

Stirling drained the last of his whisky. He addressed the frightened company commander. 'Do you think, Major, you could send a runner with us to take us to your battalion HQ? Perhaps they can supply us there with transport. We want to get back and report as soon as possible.'

The company commander put on his helmet. 'I'll take you back myself,' he said in a shaky voice and Mayne wondered how long he'd be able to stick it in the front line; the man's nerves were obviously shot to pieces.

'You'll keep a lookout for the rest of our party if they come this way,'

241

Mayne said and then without waiting for an answer turned and stared across no man's land, littered with the debris of battle—a burning tank, a wrecked 25 cwt gun, the still figures of dead Germans from the last attack, looking like a collection of abandoned children's toys. But the desert remained obstinately empty. Suddenly Mayne realized with the instant certainty of a vision, that O'Sullivan wouldn't be coming back.

Mayne shook himself, angry at the Celtic streak in him that made him see such things. It was something he disliked, but he was certain Bill was as good as dead. He turned. Wordlessly he trudged through the sand after the frightened major...

The three of them cowered in the wadi, hardly daring to breathe. The Italian cavalrymen were so close that they could smell the thick warm stable odour of their horses. But already night was beginning to sweep across the desert floor like the wings of some great silent hawk, and the three fugitives could tell by the way the horses snorted and shook their heads making their harnesses jingle, that the mounts wanted to leave before total darkness settled down on the desert.

A moment later someone gave an order and they could hear the soft 'thwacks' as the native cavalry smacked the rumps of their horses. The cavalry was leaving.

Hare breathed out hard. 'That was a close one, sir,' he whispered, as O'Sullivan carefully raised his head above the rock behind which they were hiding.

'Yes,' he answered after a moment. 'But they're off now. We'll give 'em five minutes and then we'll carry on.'

Minutes later they were on their way once more, three lone figures plodding across that endless desert, knowing that they had to make it to the British lines this night or they never would. They wouldn't be able to survive a whole day in the German front area; undoubtedly they'd be picked up sooner or later...

'I joined up in '33,' Smith 175 was saying, 'Couldn't stick the unemployment. My mum didn't want me to go, but she thought I'd be better off in the Guards. My old dad—he's dead now—he'd been a Grenadier in the first show. He was all for it, sir, of course.'

'What was the Brigade like in those days?' O'Sullivan asked, taking his eyes off the dial of his compass.

'They were some hard buggers of NCOs in those days, sir, if you'll forgive my French.'

'I will.'

'But us recruits got three square meals a

day and everything was clean and polished and sparkling. You can't imagine, sir, what that meant to an 18–year-old who had been brought up in a condemned one-up and one-down house with an outside lav, and gas lighting. God, when they first let me out in uniform at Pirbright, I did feel proud. I could have danced on air.' He grinned at the memory, his teeth a dazzling white in the darkness.

O'Sullivan smiled back at him. What a splendid fellow Smith 175 was, he told himself. Did he deserve to command men like that, with no prospects, prepared to risk their lives out here in the desert for not more than a pound a week, while back home the civvies were earning ten times that amount in cushy jobs in the war factories?

'Of course,' Smith 175 was continuing, 'I came from a tough district back in Blighty. Where I lived as a kid the men used to make funny hats for the races and dos like that.'

'Funny hats?' O'Sullivan queried.

'Yes,' Smith 175 answered. 'They'd open the brim of an old trilby and insert razor blades, with just a bit of the sharp end showing. They used them to slash fellers from rival gangs if they got uppity.'

'But why funny hats?' O'Sullivan persisted.

''Cos, they used to say that when you'd been hit by a funny hat *you ended up in stitches.*'

Smith 175 chortled at his own joke and behind them Hare sniggered.

It was the last sound he ever made, save for one long scream, as the dum-dum bullet slammed into his back and lifted him clean off his feet. When he hit the ground again he was dead.

O'Sullivan felt as if someone had hit him a great blow with a stick across his back. The very breath exploded out of his lungs. As he went down to his knees, he could already feel the hot blood trickling down the small of his back and see the red mist which was threatening to engulf him.

Smith 175 went down on his right knee cursing angrily, as he felt the sharp pain in his right side, as if someone had just poked into the flesh with a red-hot poker. But his years of training stood him in good stead. In pain as he was, he knew he couldn't just succumb. He *had* to fight back. He spun round, swaying badly as he did so. With his good arm, he raised the Tommy gun. The Italian cavalrymen—there were five of them—were clearly outlined in the silver light of the moon, as they reined their horses. They had dealt with the handful of fugitives by catching them by surprise in this manner. 'Try this one for frigging size,' Smith 175 snarled and pressed the trigger, aiming at both rider and mount.

The Tommy gun burst into frenetic life. Tracer slashed the night. Horse and rider went down in a confusion of man and beast, the horses whinnying piteously, while their riders screamed and shrieked as that merciless fire struck them.

Limping the best he could, feeling the blood trickle down his side, Smith 175 went across to where they lay in a tangled heap. Coldly, deliberately, he started to blow the back of the head off each of the trapped Italian troops. Then he fainted.

Chapter Eight

O'Sullivan was drifting in and out of consciousness... 'You are very young,' she said softly, staring down at him, her naked body coloured a soft pink in the light of the bedside lamp. 'But I shall show you something this night which you will show your woman—women—so that they can give you pleasure when you are very old.' She laughed softly, as if at some private joke.

She bent and placed her lips around his slack penis, sucking it into her mouth, which felt as if it were red-hot. Slowly, very slowly and tantalizingly, her cunning little pink tongue began to lick around the end of his penis. In and out, round and round, she flicked that artful tongue of hers till he was panting like an animal with sheer naked desire.

'You see,' she said huskily, lips scarlet and wet, as she stared at his excited young face with those mysterious dark-brown eyes of hers. 'You understand...feel the great delight of what I am doing.'

He nodded, not trusting himself to speak.

Her hand reached out, sought and found his testicles. Gently she squeezed them. He felt himself harden even more. The desire to plunge himself into her ripe body was almost unbearable. Again he was gasping and panting like a dog on heat.

'Now you know what has to be done by your woman when you grow old.' She bent over him once more and took him into her mouth. Then he was forgotten as she sucked fervently at his penis, as if her very life depended upon it...

...'Old, sir, what do you mean, sir?' It was Smith 175's voice coming from a long, long way off.

O'Sullivan opened his eyes. It was still dark and he was moving, but not under

247

his own strength. Something was carrying him, jogging up and down in a strange fashion.

In the darkness, Smith 175 seemed to read his thoughts. 'It's one of the Eyetie nags, sir,' he explained. 'It caught a packet, but it still can move—as yet.'

O'Sullivan absorbed the information with difficulty, 'where's Hare?' he asked thickly, feeling a little sick. There was an awful nagging pain in his back, too.

'Bought it, sir,' Smith 175 said laconically. 'Those Eyetie bastards had cut an X in the nose of the bullets they used. They blew poor Hare's back wide open. He died within five minutes and I got a bit of his in my side and leg.'

'Me?' O'Sullivan asked, the red mist threatening to overcome him once more.

'You took a nasty one in the back as well, sir.' Smith replied. He had used three shell dressings to try to stop the bleeding from the huge gaping wound in the young officer's back and had failed. In the end, he had urinated in some desert sand and packed the great tear with the clogged wet sand. That had stopped the bleeding, but he knew that O'Sullivan couldn't survive for long with a wound like that if he didn't receive medical treatment soon.

'But you'll make out all right—*sir?*' Smith's voice took on a new urgent tone.

248

O'Sullivan's head had lolled to one side again. 'Christ, I hope he ain't snuffed it,' Smith 175 said to himself anxiously. He bent with difficulty and listened hard.

All around was silent under the cold spectral light of the moon, save for the eerie keening of the particles of sand rubbing up and down against one another, giving off that strange night song of the desert.

He gave a sigh of relief. O'Sullivan was breathing. He was still alive. 'Thank God for that,' he said and gave the wounded beast a slap across its rump, 'Gee-up, Liza,' he urged. 'We ain't got far to go now.' He peered at the pink silent flickering to his front which he knew was the front line. 'No, not far to go now.' He started to stumble forward next to the nag carrying the wounded unconscious officer, 'Not far now,' he repeated, as if it were some kind of litany. 'Not...far...'

Empire Sunday. He was nine. The big hall was full of the O'Sullivans. Big hearty men, some in uniform, some in black suits, their shoes highly polished, chests heavy with glittering medals, dating back to the Boer War. All calling at the harassed sweating little maids for G and T's and whisky, happy that the great parade was over and they could quench their thirst at last.

249

He had loved the parade. Uncle Charles, who couldn't march because of his 'pegleg', as he called it, had placed him on his big shoulders and he had watched above the cheering, flag-waving crowd. How proud he had been of the O'Sullivans, every time he had caught glimpses of one of them: faces set, proud and fierce, as they had swung a perfect 'eyes right' at the saluting base, sweeping off their bowlers or clapping an immaculate brown-leather gloved hand to their caps. What an honour it was to belong to such a family of fine soldiers!

Now they were all there, so tall, loud and fierce, the O'Sullivans, but he wasn't frightened as he stared up at their faces flushed and tanned with years of chota pegs and service to the King-Emperor in his far flung Empire. One day he would be like that, too. Fate had ordained it for him.

They passed to and fro, patting him absently on the head, saying 'good little Billy' in their loud booming voices and telling their tales of war, 'So I said to my chaps, now chaps we're going over the top and then I saw young Fletcher. He was in an absolute funk, I can tell you. So I sez to him, who would you rather face, Fletcher, me or the Hun? He went over the top all right, killed leading his chaps half an hour later. Bullet straight through the heart. Nice clean death, what?'

'I hope you heard that, young Billy and took note of it?' It was his grandfather, General Sir William O'Sullivan, VC. Tall hawk-nosed, hair silver, with the dull maroon ribbon of the Victoria Cross at his lapel, he bent down. He smelled of whisky and hair pomade. It was the grandfather smell, he told himself. He would remember it always, even when he was as old as they all were now.

'You're getting a big boy now, Billy. One day you'll join the family regiment, the Grenadiers. God forbid there is another war. But if there is, Billy, remember this. I won't probably be there to give you this advice. So I'll give you it now. You'll be afraid at times—we all were at some time or other in our own wars.' He glared fiercely at the little boy in his Eton collar. 'But you must never let that fear show to your chaps or your fellow officers. You are an O'Sullivan—and the O'Sullivans go on to the very end. Do you understand, Billy?'

'Yes, sir,' he answered dutifully, wondering what 'to the very end' meant. It was only after his first action as an 18–year-old subaltern in France had he realized what the words had signified. They meant—to the death...

251

...'The old nag's gone and had it, sir,' Smith 175 said miserably, his voice came from far away.

O'Sullivan flickered open his eyes. The scene came into focus in the cold hard light of the moon. He lay on the cold sand with Smith 175 peering down anxiously at him. A few feet away the Italian horse lay whinnying piteously, trying to get to its hindlegs, but failing each time miserably. In the hard mercilessly light O'Sullivan could see the great wet stain of blood on its shivering flank.

'Knackered totally,' Smith 175 said, following the direction of his gaze.

'What are we going to do?' O'Sullivan asked, quite calmly, as if he had already come to accept his fate. 'I'm afraid I just can't walk, Smithie.' He looked to the east. The sky was already beginning to flush a dirty white, the sign of the false dawn. 'You can make it though,' he added.

'Sod that for a lark, sir,' Smith 175 said hotly. 'I'm not leaving you behind, sir, like we had to do with poor old Dawson. I can carry you,' Smith 175 said stoutly.

'Not for long,' O'Sullivan objected.

'For long enough, sir. The front can't be more than a couple of miles off now. I can see the flares and the usual shit going off quite clearly. I could make that even with

252

you on my back, sir, by the time both sides stand to at dawn.'

'But you're throwing away your own chances, Smithie,' O'Sullivan said miserably, trying to resist the rising temptation Smith's offer gave him.

'We both go or neither of us does,' Smith 175 said with an air of finality.

'All right then,' O'Sullivan said, feeling very weak and faint again. 'On one condition.'

'What's that, sir?'

'If you feel you can't go on still carrying me, you dump me at once. The Jerries usually treat their prisoners quite well.'

'Nobody's dumping nobody,' Smith 175 declared. With a grunt he bent down and hoisted the wounded officer onto his shoulder, biting his bottom lip till the blood came as he felt the pain surge through his wounded body. Legs feeling like jelly, he staggered on with his burden, eyes fixed longingly on the front, willing it to get closer while he still could go on...

...'I'll call you sir,' the drill instructor, whose jaw seemed to be worked by stiff metal springs snapped. He thrust his moustached, beefy face close to O'Sullivan's so that the latter could smell the odour of last night's stale beer. 'And you'll call me sir as well, till yer become an officer and gent—if yer ever do. Now mind that, we've got standards to keep at Sandhurst, sir. Do you understand, sir?' To which he replied smartly, 'Yes, sir.'

At seventeen and a half, O'Sullivan was not an imaginative or particularly sensitive boy. But the sound of a hundred pairs of hobnail boots hitting the concrete of the square at the same time, with the drill instructors bellowing, 'Company will advance. By the right, quick march' had thrilled him to the core.

For now he knew he belonged. For now he belonged to a three-hundred-year-old tradition: the tradition of the O'Sullivans. As a young man his father had been through this, as well as his uncles, the General, too. In due course, God willing, his own son would undergo it also.

'You're members of the British Army,' Staff Sergeant Firbanks would bellow at them, 'the finest army in the world. Some of you will join the Brigade of Guards—if yer lucky—the finest brigade in that army. A lucky few will be privileged to join my own regiment, the Grenadier Guards, the finest of the lot.'

Then the drill sergeant, eyes invisible under the peak of his cap, brass-bound pacing stick under his arm, would cry with that lopsided grin of his: 'Crap said the King and a thousand arseholes bent and took the strain, for in them days the words of the King was law.'

And they would grin back at him and he would shout, those invisible eyes revealing nothing, 'Wipe them cheeky grins off yer faces. This ain't no frigging Cheltenham Ladies frigging College, yer know...'

...'Crap...said the...King and...a thousand arseholes bent...' O'Sullivan choked and could go on no longer.

As quickly as he could, Smith 175 took out his khaki handkerchief, poured the last of his water from the water bottle on it and dabbed the damp cloth to O'Sullivan's brow like an anxious mother might do to a sickening baby, 'It's all right, sir,' he gasped. 'We're almost there. I'll see you across the line... Honest, sir...'

O'Sullivan gave a great shudder, his spine arching like a taut bow.

'Sir,' Smith 175 cried in alarm. 'Sir.' He dropped the handkerchief. He knew he couldn't walk and carry the officer any more, but he could crawl. Somehow he got O'Sullivan on his back, feeling the wet gore of his shattered back. O'Sullivan was bleeding through the packed sand once more. 'It's all right, sir. It won't be long now.'

With painful slowness he started to crawl forward, feeling the gravel and stone surface of the desert cut cruelly into his hands, while to his front the red signal flares started to hush into the dawn sky, signifying trouble ahead. 'It's all right...all right.'

O'Sullivan's mind was a maelstrom of pageant and ceremony, a naked woman, guardsmen stamping their boots outside Buck House, the loud blare of brass bands, a naked foreign woman sucking at his cock, as if her life depended upon it and a general looking down at him and rasping in a throaty voice, *The O'Sullivans go on to the very end.*

Then he was dead.

Chapter Nine

'Halt, who goes—' the harsh challenge broke off to be replaced by one almost of awe, 'what the frigging hell is it? Sarge, there's two of our blokes out here.'

Almost immediately half a dozen infantrymen clambered over the rampart of sandbags, dropping their weapons as they did so, rushing to the two figures sprawled in the sand. One was a big man, his tattered khaki uniform, black with caked blood. The other, who lay half sprawled over him, was younger, his face almost serene.

Gently the infantrymen carried the two of them back to the trench. Just in time. Three hundred yards away a German machine gun opened up sending a vicious burst of bullets at the spot where they had been a few moments before.

In the dugout, a middle-aged sergeant, grey-haired and wearing steel-rimmed Army issue spectacles, bent down and placed his hand in front of the younger man's mouth. Next to him the bigger man, his lips parched and cracked, his face covered with desert sores, started to open his eyes.

The middle-aged sergeant felt for the young man's neck. His hand rested there for a moment or two. But there was no pulse. He shook his head sadly. 'He's bought it,' he said to no-one in particular.

The big man, peering through the narrowed slits of his puffed-up eyes, croaked, 'What did you say, Sarge?'

The sergeant looked at him and told himself that the big man was pretty near death himself, but he'd survive if they got him to the field dressing station in time. 'He's dead,' he said tonelessly and untugging his water bottle handed it to the other man. 'Here, have a swig. There's a drop of rum in the water.'

The big man waved away the bottle weakly, as if he were angry with the offer at this moment. 'What did you say?'

The sergeant repeated his words.

'But he...can't...be,' the big man stuttered. 'After what he's been through.'

'Well, he is,' the sergeant said doggedly. He pulled off the dead man's purple beret and was about to cover the dead man's face with it, when he saw the flaming sword badge which adorned it. He frowned and peered at the unfamiliar badge through his glasses, 'What mob is this?' he asked, forgetting the dead man for a moment—he'd seen a lot of them in the last three years.

Smith 175 accepted the water bottle and took a greedy swallow before answering. 'SAS,' he said thickly.

'What's that, mate, when it's at home?' one of the curious infantrymen asked, ducking automatically as a German shell exploded a hundred yards away.

Smith 175, a new pride flushing his haggard, worn face, didn't seem to notice. He looked at the dead young officer, who had fought and died bravely because he believed implicitly in this new unit, and said, 'Special Air Service.'

'Never heard of it, mate,' the infantryman said.

'You will...you will,' Smith 175 said, as

the ambulance, box-like and camouflaged, came racing over the desert at speed to take him to the field dressing station. 'All of you will.' Suddenly, as he stared down at young O'Sullivan, dead at the age of nineteen, dead before he had started to live, his voice cracked. His shoulders started to heave and he wept.

Thus it was that, with the old sergeant's arm around his shoulder, they led Smith 175 away to the waiting ambulance, the bitter tears coursing down his worn cheeks.

'All right, lads,' the old sergeant ordered, as the ambulance raced away, 'let's plant the young officer before the Jerries start firing their bloody artillery agen.'

Half a dozen soldiers started to dig. They knew it wouldn't be long before the ambulance would be out of sight, then the Germans would commence firing once more. They dug with a will into the soft sand. In a matter of minutes they had a hole deep enough to bury the officer in.

The sergeant stooped and tugged off one of the two identity discs and put it in the pocket of his shorts. Then he covered the dead man's face with his beret. For an instant he stared at the motto beneath the flaming sword. 'Who dares, wins'. He nodded as if confirming his own thoughts about this new mob, of which the wounded giant had predicted they would hear so much. Then very businesslike, as he heard the first sharp dry crack of an 88mm cannon opening fire, he ordered, 'All right, lads cover him up-double quick time...'

He took one last look at the dead man, his face hidden by that blood-red beret. Then the sand and soil started to rain down upon the body and the first of the O'Sullivans to fight with the Special Air Service started to disappear under the earth. Slowly, a little sadly, the middle-aged sergeant straightened up and gave him a last salute...

ENVOI

'You know I think the bloody O'Sullivans will take over the SAS one bloody day.'

The Sayings of Paddy Mayne
Christmas Eve, 1941

In the big mess tent the Regiment's self-appointed choir was practising 'Silent Night' with the accompaniment of someone playing the mouth organ (badly) and another banging his spoons on jam jars filled with water (very badly).

Over at the cook tent the sweating cooks were preparing the officers' Christmas dinner, which they would eat this evening; for on the morrow they would serve the troops their breakfast in their bunks to be followed by serving them their Christmas dinner—fried spam, baked Australian potatoes out of a tin, with Yorkshire pudding made up of ground-up ration biscuits mixed with Canadian powdered milk. The troops weren't thrilled at the prospect, but the thought of two bottles of *Rheingold* beer and a half mug of issue rum afterwards cheered them up mightily.

In the orderly room, Paddy Mayne and Sergeant Smith MM., were finishing up the last of the paperwork for this December day. At the front the guns were silent, not because it was Christmas Eve, but because both the British and German Armies had run out of steam. There had been too many casualties and too much material lost. So spontaneously both friend and foe had decided to celebrate Christmas instead.

'Looks about the lot, Smithie!' Paddy Mayne exclaimed, signing the last requisition form for 'Army drawers, cellulose, soldier for the use of', and tossing down his little wooden pen. 'Christ, I never thought it'd sink to this—bloody army requisition forms.' He sighed mightily.

Smith 175 smiled sympathetically, 'These things are sent to try us, sir,' he said. 'Do you want to see the new draft from the UK now, sir? One officer and thirty other ranks, all from the Parachute Regiment.'

Paddy Mayne's craggy face brightened up. These were the first reinforcements they had received since the failed attempt on Rommel's life. He picked up his beret and said, 'Rather. They'll please the CO. He's been begging for new bodies in Cairo for over a month now. Come on, Smithie.'

'They ain't got their knees brown yet,' Smith 175 said as they went out into the thin midday winter sun, 'but they look a likely lot of lads.'

As Mayne appeared, the young officer at the front of the three ranks of volunteers, all wearing the badge of the Parachute Regiment, called them to attention and swung Paddy Mayne a tremendous salute.

As Smith 175 had said the men were pale and lacked the tan of the desert veterans, but they were tough-looking and very fit. Mayne thought Stirling would be very pleased with them; he was.

'Second Lieutenant Rory O'Sullivan,' the young officer reported, as Mayne acknowledged the salute and ordered the volunteers to stand at ease.

Smith 175's smile vanished as he heard the name. He looked at the young officer. He was bigger than poor dead Mr O'Sullivan, and his hair was a shocking Celtic red. He didn't have that worried look either that the dead officer had always worn, as if he constantly worried about his men, but there was something in the newcomer's face which was strangely familiar.

Paddy Mayne must have thought so too. Instead of giving the usual little welcoming speech he gave new recruits, he asked, 'Are you in any way related to Bill O'Sullivan who once served in the Regiment?'

The newcomer gave the craggy-faced giant Irish-man an easy, confident smile. 'Yes, Bill was my cousin. We were at Eton together, but he was ahead of me, but I didn't know him too well.' He lowered his gaze for a moment, but the smile remained on his face, 'I was kicked out at fifteen you see.'

'Kicked out?' Mayne echoed a little surprised although he had been kicked out of many places in his short life.

'Yes sir, women and booze,' the 18-year-old second-lieutenant said with a laugh.

'Well, you won't get much of either out here in this arsehole of the world.' He indicated the camp and the mess tent from which were now coming the ragged strained melody and words of 'Good King Wenceslas'.

'Didn't really come for that, sir,' O'Sullivan replied a little cheekily. 'Came for the scrap. Once we knew that our battalion wouldn't go into action till next year, I got the Governor—my father—to pull a few strings at the War House and got me sent out to you. I brought quite a few chaps with me,' he indicated the grinning paras standing at ease behind him. 'Don't think the CO liked it too much, but he had to do what the brass-hats told him. So now we're here, sir.'

He looked at Paddy Mayne winningly, as the latter gave Smith a significant look. Smith 175 smiled back and prayed that Rory O'Sullivan would last longer than his cousin and somehow he felt he would. He'd seen the kind before. They were the indestructible ones.

'Well,' Paddy Mayne said slowly, as if he were giving the matter some thought, 'we've not had two members of the same family in the Regiment before.'

'Don't give it a second thought, sir,' Rory O'Sullivan said airily. 'There's plenty of us O'Sullivans, around. Bags of 'em. If I get bumped off there'll be another one to take my place, sir.'

Smith 175 blinked away sudden tears, telling himself he was a bloody old silly woman. Over at the mess tent, the makeshift choir was singing, 'God rest ye merry gentlemen. Let nothing ye dismay...'

Paddy Mayne smiled. The sentiment seemed appropriate enough. Nothing would dismay the SAS. They had been through some bloody hard times. Now, with young blood like the cheeky, absolutely confident young subaltern coming along, things would change, he knew that implicitly.

'All right, O'Sullivan, stand your chaps down. Come over to the mess and have a noggin. It's good to have an O'Sullivan with the Regiment again.'

O'Sullivan dismissed his men and then jauntily, chatting like long lost brothers, the two giants walked over to the mess tent, while Sergeant Smith 175 stared at their retreating backs in a mixture of sadness and hope.

'God rest ye sodding gentlemen,' he said finally. He turned smartly and walked away.